# Where There's a Will

## By

## ALYSIA S. KNIGHT

Where There's a Will

By Alysia S. Knight
Published by Heart Dreams Press
Copyright © 2012 Alysia S. Knight
Cover design: by Kelli Ann Morgan @
www.inspirecreativeservices.com

ISBN:1-942000-23-5
ISBN-13:978-1-942000-23-5

# Also available from Alysia S. Knight

C3ED

Past To Die For

Temperature Rising

Kare for Me

Blind Witness

Beauty and the Chief

Trail to Her Heart

His Governess

Her Brand of Trouble

The Ruins – Out of Time

My Spy

Whistleblower

Mindblower

Beautiful Heart

C3ED

## TO MY FAMILY

Thanks for all the love and support.
Love you forever,
Alysia S. Knight

# Chapter One

"Rand, you can't go through with this." Elizabeth Carlisle Monroe pleaded.

Rand understood his mother's concern but he'd researched, planned, and his mind was made up. He straightened from the counter on which he'd been leaning. "For the last time, it wasn't my idea. It was Grandfather who made the decision for me."

"But there must be some other way," his mother objected.

"I'm aware there's another way, but I'm just not going to be trapped into it. Grandfather stipulated an heir, not a wife."

"He just wanted you happily settled."

"He wanted his own way, and though I loved him, I'm still not going to let him control me, especially from the grave. I am thirty-two years old and have been running Roe Technology for ten years. Did he really think he could get away with this dictate?" Rand had to fight to keep his frustration in.

"Then why go through it all? You don't need his company or money. You have your own interests."

"And leave Roe to the wicked step-grandmother, tweedle-da, bimbit and the wicked witch-in-making. Not a chance. They'd bleed the company dry in a month.

Grandfather put his life in it. Heck, I have put too much of my life in it. Besides, what about the employees and their families? We're talking about a couple thousand lives. I will not do that to them," he said firmly.

"What about the life of the child you create?" his mother pointed out.

"I will love and care for the child." His voice dropped to a softer tone. "Tell me, will you not love the child just because it is not conceived in the conventional way?"

"You know I will." Her shoulders drooped in resignation. "I just think it should have a mother not a …" She stopped and threw her arms up in a helpless gesture.

Rand softened, stepping forward to place his hands on her shoulders. "You're right." He met her gaze. "And I could have gone out and gotten any number of women pregnant, but there still would not have been love. We would've broken up, and the child would've been left with a single parent."

He drew in a breath when his mother failed to comment. "This way, the baby will be mine without any custody battles. And then, if I should meet a woman, fall in love and wish to marry, I will be free to do so. I haven't given up on marriage or love. I just don't see it happening before the ten-and-a-half-month deadline. It's not that I haven't thought this out. I spent the last six weeks thinking about it. I've screened dozens of young women to be a surrogate mother. The woman I've chosen is healthy, intelligent, and has legally signed all rights to the child to me. In return, I'm paying for her schooling."

He pushed his hand back through his hair, feeling frustration of his own. "I know you feel I'm being cold blooded, but this is the way it will be. Now, I have an appointment at the doctor's office. Wish me luck. If all goes well, within a couple weeks you may be expecting your first grandchild." Before his mother could object any further, he kissed her cheek and headed out the door.

 C3༔80

Kiley Adams jumped when the door to the examination room opened. Her attention went to the snowy-white-haired doctor, who had delivered her over twenty-three years earlier. She relaxed a little.

"Kiley, hello. This is a surprise." The doctor greeted her warmly.

"Hello, Dr. Matthews."

"What brings you here today?"

"I was dropping off the new floral arrangement for the waiting room." She fidgeted slightly.

"I'll have to go take a look at it later. Laura keeps remarking about the one you did for our entry, and how you were absolutely right about the colors and shape. She loves it."

"I'm glad." Kiley felt the normal rush of pleasure she experienced when people liked her arrangements.

"Now, what can I do for you?"

"I was talking with Delores out front and mentioned that I have a cold I can't seem to shake. She insisted I have it checked."

Dr. Matthews laughed. "It's nice to know my nurse is drumming up business for me, but I bet you won't mention when you don't feel well to her again." He always liked to tease her. "Well, let's look at you." He proceeded with the exam. "Take a deep breath. Another. How are you handling things with your grandmother gone?" he asked as he listened to her lungs.

"I miss her," Kiley said softly.

"She was a good woman, but she was sick for a long time. Elcie hated that she was a burden to you."

"She was never a burden. She raised me and I loved her."

"I know, dear. But still there are not many people who would've done what you did."

"There wasn't any other choice."

7

"Not many nineteen-year-olds would have given up their dreams of college to take over financial and physical care for an aging grandmother with multiple sclerosis. You did a wonderful job of it."

Embarrassed, Kiley had to fight not to squirm as he looked in her ears.

Luckily, he changed the subject. "You have a slight ear infection and your throat is inflamed. I can give you a shot or prescription that will help."

"I'll take the shot."

"All right. You know, your chart here shows you have never had a Pap smear. We really ought to do one."

"I'm leaving town for a week and a half to house sit."

"It only takes a few minutes. We could do it right now while you're here."

"Oh." There was no stopping the blush that warmed her cheeks.

Dr. Matthews patted her knee fondly. "There's really nothing to it. The nurse practitioner can do it if you prefer having someone you don't know." He tried to soothe her.

"I ... can it wait?"

"Well, it really isn't critical, but you should've had one by your age. It would be for the best," he instructed.

"I really think I'd rather wait."

"All right, but if you change your mind, just come in at any time. Don't worry about making an appointment. Just tell Delores I said so."

"You think I should have one?"

"Yes, there's nothing to worry or be embarrassed about. Think about it." He counseled in the same gentle way he had her grandmother for years.

She nodded.

"All right, Delores will be in with the antibiotic. Get plenty of rest, and keep in touch." He gave her knee another pat before hurrying off to the next room.

Cঊৎৡঌ

Rand felt uncomfortable entering the women's center. It was a feeling he wasn't accustomed to. The waiting room was filled with women. There was only one other man, who waited by his very pregnant wife. Rand shifted around looking for Rebecca, the second year college student he'd chosen to be the surrogate mother. It still shocked him how easy it had been to find a young woman willing to have his child.

"Mr. Monroe." The tremor in the voice was strong.

He turned. By the time he was in his early mid-twenties, people tended to address him formally. At thirty-two – it was commonplace.

"Rebecca," he greeted. "I'll get us signed in." He watched the girl fidget. "You seem nervous."

"Yes, sir."

"It'll soon be over."

He moved away. Soon. Actually, it would be nine months, if it worked the first time. And nervous – she definitely was not the only nervous one. As he stepped away from the sign-in desk, the inner door opened smacking him in the forehead.

"Oh, excuse me. I … I'm terribly sorry."

Rand found himself looking into the most incredible blue eyes he'd ever seen. They were framed by long lashes that were naturally dark. The rest of the beautiful face seemed to be just as clean and natural, except for the lips, which were glossed a soft, dewy rose.

"Are you all right?" The eyes flickered over his face. Her hand followed his to the bump forming on his forehead.

"Oh, I'm sorry." She jerked back her hand self-consciously, leading him to believe she felt the same jolt on contact that he had. "How embarrassing," she stammered. Her gaze finally left his to drop to the floor, letting a golden veil of hair fall forward to hide her face.

Immediately, he gathered his senses, or at least tried. "I'm fine. It's all right." Rand tried to reassure her.

Her eyes came back up. "I'm so sorry."

"It was an accident." He gave a smile to ease her. "No harm done."

"You're certain?" She stepped back.

He felt the loss of her nearness but nodded.

Her lashes fluttered down. "Sorry," she whispered again and was gone in a dash for the door.

The world that had seemed to stop picked back up, but no one else seemed to notice what had occurred. He looked back to the door through which she departed. A sense of loss washed over him. He shook it away. She wasn't his to lose.

Unable to stop his thoughts, he wondered why she was here. What had her distracted? He would like to say "he had" but couldn't. He hoped nothing was wrong. As his eyes rested on the pregnant women in the office, then on Rebecca who was about to be inseminated, he felt amiss. He wondered if the blue-eyed beauty had just found out she was pregnant. Was some lucky man about to find out he was going to be a father?

ᘓᙄ

Kiley tried to settle her racing heart. Not entirely sure what disturbed her. She couldn't believe her reaction to the man who was most likely married. Married and waiting for his pregnant or possibly sick wife. She hoped for his sake, not the latter. Having someone you loved ill was sad. Then again, so was being too big of a chicken to have a Pap smear. It was an ordinary medical test women had every day.

She paced back and forth on the sidewalk. There was nothing, nothing at all to be nervous about. Just because she was nearly twenty-four years old and had never been touched or exposed.

Heavens, if her grandmother were here, she'd call her a ninny and tell her to get right back in there. Kiley looked up to see her bus coming, but knew she wouldn't be getting on it. A few minutes later, she was back inside the doctor's office, and Dolores, Dr. Matthews nurse, had her waiting in the hall for the next open room.

Dr. Matthews stopped to quickly explain he'd been called to the hospital and that his nurse practitioner would do the Pap smear and everything would be all right. When she tried to say she'd come back another time, he hushed her, saying he probably wouldn't be able to get her back in again. Which, she had to admit was probably true, and it was better to just get it over with. Then he instructed his nurse to make sure it was done.

CRBO

This better work, Rand cursed. He sure didn't want to go through it again. He wondered how the beautiful blue-eyed, blonde would feel if she knew that it was his thoughts of making love to her that had done the trick, when all of the other things they had there to help arouse him hadn't. What would her husband or boyfriend say, but it didn't matter. No one else would ever know.

He felt a stab of regret. He wished that she would be carrying his baby. Rand shook his head at the unreasonably strong yearning to be able to wake up to her sweet smile every morning and fall asleep with her every night. He shifted, he was going to get aroused again.

He tried to relax and tell himself he was doing the right thing. He did want the child. Truth be told, he wanted the child very much. He liked the idea of being a father. He just would have preferred it to be with a wife – one that he loved. He could shoot his grandfather for putting him into such an awkward position. His grandfather knew how much he loved the company he'd run for years. He cursed again under his breath.

CRBO

For the second time in just over an hour, Kiley sat on an examination table. This time nude from the waist down covered with only a paper sheet. Dolores warned her it might be a wait and to just relax.

*Relax, hah.* She was ready to chicken out again. When the lights went out, Kiley knew it was a sign. She was already climbing off the table to get dressed and flee when Delores popped back in with a flashlight for her and to say the power was out, but everything was all right. They would wait for the power to come back on or do it by flashlight.

Kiley waited, deciding maybe it was less embarrassing to have it done in the dark. She let out a squeak of surprise when the doctor burst inside, pushing a small metal tray with one hand. The glimpse she got of the instruments on the tray looked torturous. Then she couldn't see anything as the powerful flashlight he carried in his other hand caught her in the eyes.

"Where's the nurse?" the man demanded in a highly irritated tone.

"I ... I don't know."

"Never mind, we can't wait. Just lay back," he ordered. "There's no need to waste time."

There was a sharp bang of metal against the table.

Kiley jumped.

"Feet up in the stirrups." A cold hand gripped her ankle forcing one foot into place then doing the same to the other. "The nurse should've had you ready." He swore at the dark. "Lights go out and everyone panics. Incompetence!"

"Have you ever done this in the dark?" Kiley found her voice shaky.

"No, but I could do it with my eyes shut."

*That's the only way I'd do it.* Kiley thought, closing hers. She felt a hand and tightened.

"Relax, you're tense. It won't hurt." His command didn't help, but she tried. "You know what to expect."

Kiley almost said no, she didn't, but flinched instead. She took a deep breath and counted away the minutes to ignore what was happening.

"You'll feel the swabbing now," he said. "There. That should do. We'll know the results in a couple of days. Stay still for a while, then you can get dressed. You should take it easy today. Lay down and rest." With that he left, totally dismissing her.

After a few minutes, Kiley stopped shaking and hurried to dress. "That wasn't too bad," she said out loud to herself. Still, glad it was over, she made her escape. The darkened hallway gave her cover as she headed for the exit sign. She knew it was foolish, but she didn't want to see anyone.

Relief flowed over her when the light coming in the windows revealed no people waiting. Hurrying past the nurse's desk, she collided with a male body that stepped into her path. For the second time that day, she looked up into the man's gray eyes. This time they seemed stormy and more disturbing.

For a minute, she was caught in his gaze then, like a startled rabbit, she fled. Forcing her thoughts from the doctor's office and the man, she ran to catch the bus. She had less than two hours to be at the Rasmussens' to housesit and clean for the next ten days.

ଔଞ

Rand paced back and forth. *Of all the times for the power to fail.* He clinched his jaw, thinking of Dr. Harvey's attempt to appease him with the crude remark that most babies were made in the dark. He was really beginning to dislike the man. Why had he stayed with Harvey? The man reminded him of an old-time, snake-oil salesman – without the charm. Highly recommended as he was, Rand wished it wasn't too late to get someone else.

The outside door opened and to his surprise Rebecca walked in. "Rebecca. How'd you get out there?"

"I snuck out the back to go for a walk." Her hands were clasped in front of her and she kept wringing them in her agitation. "Mr. Monroe, I'm sorry, I can't do it. I thought I could, but I can't. My boyfriend David – well we've only been dating a couple of weeks, but I think he's the one, he really didn't like the idea, and I realized, even if he isn't the one, I can't do this. I'm so sorry." She ran the sentence together in her nervousness.

For a minute, Rand was too stunned to know what to say. Then he realized there was nothing he could say. It was her body – he couldn't force her to be a surrogate. He swallowed hard. At least, he had a couple of other possible candidates on his list.

"I understand. Do you have a ride home?"

She nodded. "I already called David. He's coming to get me."

Rand nodded. "I better talk to Dr. Harvey."

"I'm sorry." Tears ran down the girl's face to attest to her emotions.

He nodded and reached out to squeeze her hand.

Unable to do anything else, he walked down the dark hallway leading to a pool of light where several nurses sat at a desk. Not finding Dr. Harvey at the first desk, he continued on to the next nurse's station. There, Dr. Harvey was writing on a chart.

"We have a problem," Rand said approaching the man.

The doctor looked up scowling.

"She can't go through with it."

"It's a little late now."

"Can we save the semen?" Rand asked hopefully.

"I used most of it."

"Used?" A stab of ice pierced him.

"Of course," the doctor replied haughtily.

"Wait a minute, but …" Fear hit him like a ton of bricks. Trotting back down the hall, he found Rebecca still there. "Rebecca!"

"Yes, Mr. Monroe?" The young woman jerked her head up, startled.

"Did Dr. Harvey inseminate you?"

"No, I told you, I went for a walk."

Rand's temper soared. He turned back to the doctor who had followed him down the hall. Harvey started to stammer as soon as he met Rand's gaze.

"Now, now I assure you I inseminated the girl. The tray is still in the room." He pointed around the corner.

Rand took off in that direction almost running into another doctor coming down the hall.

"Excuse me," they both said at the same time.

"Dolores." The doctor looked past him to the next nurses' desk. "Where is Doctor Matthew's patient?"

"In eighteen," the nurse answered.

"No, she's not," the doctor said.

"Don't tell me she left." Dolores headed toward them. Rand, the two doctors and nurse converged on the same room.

Rand spun toward Dr. Harvey, grabbing the front of his white coat. "You inseminated the wrong woman."

"There's … there's some mistake." Harvey once more stumbled over the words.

"Yeah, and you made it," Rand shot back.

"But the tray was there, the woman …" The man struggled for an explanation as his words petered out. For once, his superior attitude slipped.

"What woman?" the nurse cut in. "What tray?"

"Who was in this room?" Rand asked.

"One of Dr. Matthews' patients," the nurse answered, eyeing him with caution.

"What is her name?" Rand wanted to yell.

"I can't tell you that. It's classified," the nurse answered firmly.

"I need her name!" Rand had always been able to control his anger, but for once he could feel it getting away from him.

"I can't give you that information without authorization. You'll have to contact Dr. Matthews." The nurse didn't waver.

Rand held in the next phrase that wanted to escape, and took a deep breath. "Can you get a hold of Dr. Matthews then?"

"He got called to surgery."

Rand shoved his fingers into his hair. "Can you get a message to have him contact me? It's an emergency."

The nurse finally realized something serious was up and nodded.

For a moment all Rand could think about was another man's wife pregnant with his baby. He pressed his head back against the wall and shut his eyes. A minute later the nurse was back. He opened his eyes.

"I left the message with the operating room," she said

"Thank you."

She nodded.

"Can you at least tell me, if you know?" Rand asked hurriedly before she turn away. "Is she married?"

After a moment of silence, the nurse answered a soft, "No."

"No, you can't tell me or no, not married?" Rand asked for clarification.

"No, not married." Compassion filled the woman's face.

Rand felt a bit of relief.

"What was she in for?" Was the next question he couldn't help asking?

There was another pause. "A Pap smear."

"She got a lot more than that," Rand commented, his voice full of sarcasm.

By the time Dr. Matthews got back, Rand's frustration had him ready to explode. He paced the doctor's office like a caged tiger. Fortunately, Dr. Harvey had the good sense to disappear. Otherwise, Rand was afraid he would've throttled the man.

Rand swallowed hard when he heard Dr. Matthews leave a message for the woman, Kiley, to call him.

Matthews turned to him. The man had been the epitome of calm competence since he returned to his office and learned what happened. "There was no answer at her house," the man said unnecessarily.

"What about a cell phone?" Rand fought to keep a tight rein on his own composure.

"I'm afraid she doesn't have one. She cancelled it after her grandmother passed away to conserve money. She lives on a tight budget, doing an array of odd jobs. She said she was going out of town to housesit for the next ten days."

As the doctor talked, it was obvious he held the woman in high regard, but it brought Rand no comfort. All he could think of was an unknown woman out there, possibly pregnant with his baby.

# Chapter Two

After ten days, it felt good to be home. The Rasmussens were back from their cruise, their house was cleaned spotless from top to bottom, and Kiley was a lot closer to being finished paying off her grandmother's final expenses.

Two more months and she'd have it all paid, then she could get her old car fixed and splurge on a new outfit. Not anything fancy, just new. After, she could start saving up to take a few college classes on small business management. First things first, she had to take care of her flowers.

It wasn't until lunch that she went through the messages and heard the one from Dr. Matthews. Her heart dropped at the message.

*"Kiley, this is Dr. Matthews. Can you give me a call as soon as you get this?"*

Her thoughts went to the Pap smear. Something was wrong.

The nausea she'd been feeling since the day before came back with a vengeance. Kiley dropped the phone and fled to the bathroom where she proceeded to lose her lunch.

A few minutes later she fought for calm as she walked back to the phone. Shaking, she wiped tears from her eyes and dialed Dr. Matthews's number. She was only on hold a minute, before he came on the line.

"Kiley, you got my message."

"Yes, Dr. Matthews." She couldn't keep her voice from trembling.

"Kiley, are you all right?" Concern came through the phone.

"Yes, is there something wr…wrong with my Pap smear?"

"No, dear, there is nothing wrong with that. Don't even concern yourself about it, but I do need to see you as soon as possible. Can you come in to my office this afternoon?"

"I guess so."

"Good. How about three o'clock? Is that all right?"

"Yes, I'll be there." Her voice still quivered.

"Now, don't worry. It will be just fine," he assured her.

Kiley put down the phone and stared at it. He said everything would be fine, but then what was so urgent. She lay back in the chair and closed her eyes, willing herself not to cry. It did no good to cry, especially when you didn't know the reason. She learned that with her grandmother's illness.

She could almost hear her grandmother say, *"Don't go borrowing trouble."* Well, she had an hour to work on flower arrangements before she had to get ready to meet Dr. Matthews.

 CR80

The funny feeling of being watched she'd been having since she left her house was back as Kiley stepped off the bus across the street from the Medical Plaza. Her nerves were on edge, she thought as she hurried to join the crowd at the corner waiting for the light to change. Directly across the street, an ambulance sat in front of the hospital. On the other corner was the women's clinic.

Oddly, unlike many people, Kiley didn't mind hospitals and doctors' offices, but then Dr. Matthews had been an old family friend of her grandmother's. He had been her doctor from the moment he delivered her. She also didn't have the bad experience of being at the hospital when her parents died in the car accident. Their deaths had been immediate, not prolonged in the hospital, and she had been at her grandparents' house when it happened.

More people gathered at the corner. Kiley was standing next to the curb staring at the red hand across the walk when she felt the hand on her back and the shove. She threw her arms out, grabbing for the signpost, but the momentum sent her off the curb.

People screamed.

A horn blew.

Kiley hit the ground hard. Gravel bit into her hands and knees. Tires screeched. An engine roared. Dust covered her as the huge wheels and heavy metal bumper of the bus came to stop inches from her.

Time stood still. She stared at the set of wheels. Another hand touched her back, she jerked. Realizing she'd forgot to breathe, she gulped in air.

"Easy miss, just stay still. Help will be right here."

Kiley looked up. A policeman knelt next to her. People gawked behind him, some with shocked stares, a few had cellphones up taking pictures.

The thought of her picture showing up on the news spurred her into action. "I'm, I'm all right." The words trembled out as she tried to push herself off the pavement.

"Best not move." The officer tried to keep her down.

"No, no. I'm really fine," she insisted as she stood then wobbled.

The officer caught her arm. "Maybe we better get you to the hospital to have you checked out."

"No, that's not necessary. I'm just a little shaky," Kiley assured him.

"Let me get the bus out of the way and the people cleared. You shouldn't stand close enough to the edge to slip off," the officer cautioned softly.

"I didn't slip." Kiley jerked her head around to look at him. "Someone pushed me."

Skepticism crossing his face pulled up Kiley's anger, giving her a much needed burst of adrenaline to steady herself.

"Someone pushed me," she repeated firmly.

"All right, sit here while I ask around." He directed her to the bus stop bench.

After a few minutes, it became clear no one noticed anything before she fell. The best description was from the bus driver who had observed the cluster of people waiting around the stop, then her jetting out from the group. Even with her frantic grab for the pole, he'd been certain he was going to hit her.

Still, it seemed impossible the bus missed her. Kiley dabbed the blood from her hands and knees with a tissue from her purse. Her nylons were ruined, her dress was filthy, but at least she wasn't bus mush. The adrenaline was fading, and she started to tremble again. A tear escaped to trickle down her cheek as the policemen approached.

"I'm afraid no one saw anything." His words confirmed what she already deduced.

"But someone pushed me," she repeated in another attempt to make him believe her.

He shrugged. "It may be that someone accidentally bumped in to you."

"It wasn't a bump. There was a definite hand on my back."

"We have no witnesses. Do you have anyone who would want to hurt you?" he asked.

"Well, no."

"Any enemies?"

"No."

"All right, I'll fill out a report. If you think of anything you can let me know." He handed her a card. "Are you sure you wouldn't like to go to the emergency room to be checked out?"

"No, I was on the way to my doctor's. Oh." She looked at her watch. "I'm late now."

The officer helped her to stand. As the light changed, she hurried across the street, though each step caused little shoots of pain in her knees and a dull ache in her hip that had taken the majority of her fall.

ᴄꙅᴆᴑ

Rand paced Dr. Matthews's office. The room was spacious, decorated in navy and natural tones. Two leather wingback chairs faced the large maple desk. Medical books filled the wall bookcase behind it. Wood blinds accented a window which filled the room with light. Diplomas and plants framed the door. A comfortable room, much like Rand's office, but Rand wasn't comfortable. He hadn't been for the last ten days.

Since Dr. Matthew's call, he'd been even more on edge. It had taken all his efforts to convince the doctor he had a right to be at the appointment. He had arrived ten minutes early, now it was fifteen minutes past. He paced and cursed his grandfather, then himself for this mess.

"I can't imagine what is keeping her. Kiley is usually very prompt." Dr. Matthews tried to soothe him.

"She's a woman." Dr. Harvey supplied a cutting comment. He had breezed in, out of breath, ten minutes earlier. "I don't know what all this fuss is about. The odds of her being pregnant are astronomical. Think how perfect we have to plan this process, and it still can take months to achieve. We know Mr. Monroe was clean so she won't get anything from him. Why bother."

"Because she was inseminated with my sperm, and we don't know the possibilities." Rand bit back, annoyed at the doctor's attitude. There was a soft knock at the door and Dolores opened it.

"Ah, here she is." Matthews stood, coming around his desk.

Rand turned to the door. As soon as he saw the long, wheat-colored strands of her hair, he knew her eyes would be large, clear sky-blue. It was the woman from that day, the one on his mind, in his dreams, the only one who seemed to be able to wrench his mind from the disaster of an unknown woman possibly pregnant with his child.

"Dear, what happened?" Matthews took an arm, directing her to a chair.

Rand came up from behind and noticed she was slightly unsteady. There was a tear in the hem of her blue floral dress and scraped flesh on her knees. "Are you all right?"

She jerked toward him. "Yes, I just had a little accident on the street." She sounded shaky and breathless.

"Let's see." Dr. Matthews crouched in front of her.

"I stopped at the restroom to wash them off already."

"Yes, well, we'll have Delores clean them a little better before you leave. Are you injured anywhere else?"

"No. Just scrapes and a few bruises."

"Good, can we get on with this?" The brisk voice caused her to look up, shocked at the other man who still remained seated in the room.

Kiley failed to recognize the man, but his voice she remembered as the doctor—or nurse practitioner, Dr. Matthews had mentioned. *Good thing he wasn't a doctor. He had no bedside manner.* By Dr. Matthews scowl, it was evident he thought the same thing.

Fear again rose in her. Again she looked back to Dr. Matthews. "Is there something wrong with me?"

"No, Kiley. I told you not to worry about that. You're beautifully healthy. But there is another problem. First, let me introduce Randall Monroe and Dr. Harvey. Do you mind if they're here?"

She glanced at the other doctor. *So much for bedside manner.* She couldn't keep back the thought before turning her attention back to Dr. Matthews. She shook her head.

Deep frown lines creased his brow. He pushed his hands through his snowy-white hair, and leaned back on his desk. "I don't know how to tell you this but straight out. There was a mistake made the other day. A mix up. You were not given at Pap smear."

"I don't understand. You …" She looked at Dr. Harvey then back to Dr. Matthews. "Then what?"

"When the lights went out, there was some confusion. You were mixed up with another patient and given the procedure by Dr. Harvey that was meant for them."

"Then …" She cut off as her voice broke.

"Kiley," Dr. Matthews reached out and took her hands. "The procedure was an artificial insemination."

Her trembling intensified to the point she couldn't say anything.

"Do you understand the significance?" he asked gently.

Kiley could only nod.

"We need to run some tests."

"You … you think I'm … I'm pregnant." The ringing in her ears multiplied with the pounding of her heart. The world drifted off into a haze. She tried to concentrate on the words Dr. Matthews was saying but couldn't get past 'pregnant'.

"The odds are against it, but we have to make sure. Kiley, Kiley I want you to take a couple of deep breaths," he instructed and waited until she did. "Are you okay, now?"

She thought it was an absurd question, but nodded.

"All right, I need to ask you some questions. We might not need to worry at all." Dr. Matthews moved behind his desk. Settling in the chair, he opened her file. "Have you had your menstrual cycle since you were here?"

Kiley glanced at the men on either side of her and shook her head. "No," she whispered.

"I know these are personal questions, dear, but don't be embarrassed. When do you expect your next period?"

"Today or tomorrow, maybe the next day." She blushed.

"How far apart is your cycle?"

She glanced toward Randall Monroe. Not understanding why she felt so embarrassed. They were medical personal after all – it was normal to them. "Twenty-one to twenty-two days."

"That's from the end of one to the start of the next?" Dr. Matthews asked.

"No." The answer quivered out. "Start to start."

Dr. Harvey cursed aloud. Kiley thought he muttered something like. "A baby machine."

A sobbing breath slipped from her.

"Dr. Harvey!" Dr. Matthews raised his voice.

"Shut up." Mr. Monroe snapped at Harvey then moved to kneel beside her. "This is not her fault." He slid his arm around her, turning her into him. At once she felt sheltered. She pressed her face into his shoulder.

"It's all right, dear," Dr. Matthews said comforting.

Taking a deep, calming breath, Kiley lifted her head, fighting for composure.

"How long does your normal period last?" Dr. Matthews continued.

"Five days."

Matthews turned to write on the paper. "How have you been feeling?"

"My cold cleared up, and I felt better after a day or so, but the last couple of days kind of tired. You said I needed rest, though. I haven't been sick … until today, but I was nervous after you called. I thought something was wrong. You think I'm pregnant?" She repeated her earlier question, trying to sense his answer.

Dr. Matthews looked back at her. A weight seemed to descend on him. He sighed heavily. "I won't lie to you, Kiley. I think the chances are high that it is possible."

"But I can't," her objection burst out, "I've never even …." She stopped, a blush burning her cheeks. Nausea threatened to rise again.

"I need to give you an examination and have some blood work done. Then we'll know." Dr. Matthews was gentle, trying to soothe her.

Kiley did the only thing she could – she nodded. Matthews reach over the desk and pressed the intercom button on the phone. A few seconds later, Delores opened the door. Dr. Matthews came around the desk and stretched out his hand as Randall Monroe helped her stand, handing her over to the doctor and nurse.

Kiley immediately missed his comforting arm around her.

"Delores, I want the blood work done immediately. Have someone take it to the lab and wait."

The nurse nodded and led Kiley from the room. At the doorway, she looked back at the man who had comforted her. She wished she could go back to his arms. Instead, biting her bottom lip, she followed Delores.

# Chapter Three

As soon as the door closed, Rand turned on Dr. Harvey. "You impregnated a virgin! How could you miss that? You had examined Rebecca."

"It was dark. I was doing it all by flashlight. We didn't want to wait too long and risk the sperm," the doctor said in defense. He almost sounded like a whiney little boy.

"Well, you might want to hope you mishandled it. It could save you a lot."

"With miss bunny, I wouldn't count on it." The doctor smirked.

Clinching his fist, Rand stepped toward the insolent man. "Don't you say another word about her. She's the victim here."

"Gentlemen, gentlemen, please," Dr. Matthews broke in. "You are hardly acting like professionals here. Mr. Monroe, I appreciate your concern for Kiley, but this is hardly helping her. Now, if you'll excuse me, I'll go see to her." He left the room, sending a disapproving look at Harvey on his way out.

Rand paced. Every time he thought of Kiley's pale face, eyes watery with tears, he wanted to slam his fist into Harvey's face. And when he thought of the beautiful young woman, a virgin, and pregnant with his child, he felt like he had been punched.

Luckily, Dr. Harvey wisely kept his mouth shut and stayed in his chair out of Rand's way. An eternity passed before Dr. Matthews walked in, crossed the room and sat at his desk.

"Dr. Matthews?"

"Kiley will be about five minutes, she's just getting dressed."

"Is she…?" The not knowing was killing Rand.

"We'll know for certain when we get the blood test back."

"Come on, Milton," the other doctor complained. "At this point, any second year med student can tell by a physical exam."

The older doctor rested his elbows on the desk, and steepled his fingers. "It has only been ten days, but yes. There are signs. I'm almost certain Kiley's pregnant."

Rand couldn't stop the elation from running through his body. He was going to be a father. Dr. Harvey's next words jolted him back down to earth.

"I'll take care of it this evening."

Matthews reacted before Rand could. "Now, wait a minute. If you're talking abortion, no one is going to hurry that girl into anything. True, she didn't expect any of this. But, I know her, and how she feels about life. I honestly don't believe Kiley will terminate the baby. But," he stressed the word. "The choice will be hers." He looked toward Rand pointedly. "And no one else's."

The three men all sat in quiet thought until there was a knock on the door, and Delores escorted Kiley back into the room. The nurse paused to hand Dr. Matthews a folder.

When Kiley hesitated by the door, Rand stood and stepped to her. Taking her hand in one of his, careful of the bandage now there, he slid his other arm around her, and led her to the chair. The hand that rested in his was cold and not at all steady. The young woman that seemed vibrant when he first saw her, now seemed frail and vulnerable. He held her tight against him in a half hug for reassurance before he lowered her to the chair.

Kiley settled in the chair profoundly missing the comfort of Mr. Monroe's arm. She wondered what he would have done if she had turned and buried her head into his chest as she wanted to. She wondered what she would have done. She couldn't believe she even contemplated it.

It wasn't like her to be so forward. It wasn't like her to feel so unsettled. Her grandparents had raised her to be practical, and that was how she had always been. She handled what came along, worked hard, and always tried to make the best of situations.

Well, this was way outside her realm of things to handle. She'd dreamed of having children, but she'd planned on having a husband first and certainly never considered it without being made love to first.

Dr. Matthews was talking, but she had trouble concentrating on his words until he said it was positive, no question about it. Kiley couldn't move, couldn't think. Somewhere around her someone swore harshly. From over her shoulder, another voice ordered "quiet". She felt a warm, reassuring hand on her shoulder.

"Kiley," Dr. Matthews knelt in front of her.

"I can't be. I'm not married." Kiley heard the denying words come out of her mouth over the ringing in her ears.

"Kiley, take a couple of breaths," Dr. Matthews commanded softly.

Kiley followed his directions, and her head cleared but she still felt faint. "What am I going to do? I can't have a baby." She hadn't realized she said the words out loud until Dr. Harvey spoke beside her.

"I can take care of it tonight. By tomorrow, there won't be anything to worry about."

"Harvey!" Mr. Monroe's voice sounded threatening.

That was when she realized what Dr. Harvey was talking about.

"No!" Filled with fury, Kiley stood so fast she almost knocked Dr. Matthews down. Her hands went protectively to her stomach. "You will not kill the baby."

"Be reasonable. You don't want a baby. It's hardly more than a dot right now. It's simple."

"No!" Kiley yelled, cutting him off. Tears broke free, trickling down her cheeks. She wanted to cover her ears so she couldn't hear another word. She turned away and found her face pressed into the crisp white shirt, covering the firm chest she thought of moments earlier. Strong arms locked around, sheltering her.

"Get out of here, Harvey. You've done enough." The harsh words from Mr. Monroe rumbled around her body, but they didn't frighten her.

Kiley wasn't sure how much time had passed when the heartbeat under her ear steadied. Cocooned in the warmth of a man's arms, she wondered if it was how the baby would feel in her womb, listening to her heartbeat.

"A baby." She whispered it, trying the sound of it out to herself. It sounded foreign, but a little thrill tingled through her. She wouldn't be alone. The next instant, she was filled with tribulation as her emotions yo-yoed.

"Dr. Matthews," Delores said from the doorway. "Dr. Armstrong needs you if at all possible."

At the interruption, Kiley lifted her head. She could see the indecision on the doctor's face. "I'm fine, you can go." She pulled herself up straight and stepped from Mr. Monroe's embrace. After a second, Dr. Matthews left.

Kiley looked around the room, totally overwhelmed. *A baby, her.* It seemed impossible. More impossible was Dr. Harvey's suggestion of ending its life. Life was precious. She pressed her hand to her stomach once again. Trying to take in that there was really a life there.

"Are you all right? Are you going to be sick?" The low tones washed over her, reminding Kiley of the man she'd been clinging to a moment earlier.

"Oh, no." Embarrassed, she didn't know what to say. She had clung to the man. Someone she didn't even know.

"So you don't want to have an abortion?" his next questioned jarred her.

"I couldn't."

"No one would blame you. This wasn't your choice. What happened would be considered more like a rape."

Kiley flinched. "I still couldn't," she said firmly.

"You should get a lawyer," he counseled.

"A lawyer?" That shocked her.

"Yes, Dr. Harvey was negligent in the worst way."

For the first time, she really let herself look at the man. When she'd seen him before, he had been dressed casually in Khakis and a navy shirt. He'd been appealing to her. Now, he wore the charcoal-gray suit that Kiley could tell was expensive, a brilliant, snowy-white shirt, and a burgundy and blue silk tie. He was devastatingly handsome, but for some reason, she realized he wasn't a doctor.

"Are you Dr. Harvey's lawyer?"

"No!" he stated firmly as if he didn't even want to be associated with the doctor. "No, I'm not a lawyer. I'm the fool that hired him."

"You work for the clinic?"

"No." He shifted as if uncomfortable. "I guess you could say that I'm the baby's father. It was my sperm you received." He dropped his eyes to her stomach and her hand still there.

"Oh," Kiley was shocked, not sure what to say. "That's what you were doing there that day. Your wife ..." For the first time, Kiley thought of the other side. "Oh, my." Her hand came reflexively to her mouth. "She must ... I'm sorry."

Rand took the couple of steps that separated them and caught her hands as they flittered in front of her, wrapping them firmly in his. "Calm down. It's all right. I'm not married."

Confusion rushed through Kiley. "Not married, your girlfriend."

"No, no girlfriend either." He paused. "It's a long, drawn-out story, but sufficient to say, I wanted a child and hired a young woman to be a surrogate. Only there was a mistake. You don't have to worry. If you're willing to carry the child, I will take full responsibility, financially and otherwise."

"Otherwise, as in give up the baby to you?" she said uncertainly.

"You didn't choose this. I understand."

"No, I didn't, but I don't know … I mean … I don't think, even if …" Kiley couldn't seem to get the words to come out.

"Easy. Take a deep breath."

The breath she took wasn't steady. "I'm sorry. I don't think I can just give up the baby. It's part of me. Even if you were married … I don't know what I'd do, but …" Again, unconsciously, her hand covered her stomach. "I won't deny you custody. I know the baby is from you, too. And you wanted it. But, please, don't ask me to give it up either."

Rand looked into the pleading blue eyes and knew he couldn't deny her anything. "I won't ask you to. We'll share custody. I'll have the papers drawn up."

"Papers?"

"Documents. I want this legal."

"I don't have a lawyer."

"It's okay, Kiley. I will take care of you." The words came out a promise, soft and firm.

Kiley wasn't sure why, maybe it was the way he said her name, or the sincerity she thought she saw in his eyes, but she trusted him. Kiley thrust out her hand, he looked at it a second before taking it in his to shake. A smile crested his lips.

She felt an overpowering connection to him and wondered if he felt it, too, because he lingered in releasing her hand. When he did, she swayed, suddenly light-headed.

"Easy." He caught her arms. "You better sit down. You have had quite a day."

"That's to say the least. Actually, I think I need to eat. I was feeling fine this morning but got sick after Dr. Matthews called. I thought maybe it was left over from my cold, or maybe it was a touch of flu. I'm rambling."

"Sit down." He eased her into the chair.

"The next bus will be here soon. I need to go," Kiley protested weakly.

"I'll take you home."

"You don't need to. I'm used to taking the bus. My car is old and not very reliable."

"I'll see you home. Besides, Dr. Matthews will want to talk to us before you leave."

"I–"

He cut her off by touching her arm. "I'll take you home. Please."

She looked in his eyes and found herself nodding. "I live out in the Oaks area."

"Perfect. You're on my way. I live in Castle estates."

"Oh." Kiley swallowed. She had only been in the area a couple of times, delivering custom floral arrangements. It was an elite area with huge homes, mansion-like houses that sat on several acre lots with tennis courts, swimming pools, and gardens Kiley could only dream of but was glad she didn't have to tend.

"My family originally owned a lot of the land there, but part of it was sold off over time. I built a house a year ago. I haven't got around to decorating it yet. I'm just doing it a little at a time."

She nodded, not sure what to think. Maybe not idle rich, but rich enough to pay a woman to have his baby? That led to another thought. "Mr. Monroe?"

"Rand, please." When she hesitated, he gave her a crooked grin. "Don't you think you should at least be on a first-name basis with the father of the baby you carry?"

Kiley's breath caught.

He leaned toward her. "Are you all right?"

She closed her eyes, not opening them until she felt steadier. "I'm just still trying to work it out in my mind that I could possibly be pregnant. I always wanted to have children but ..." Her chin quivered, she bit her bottom lip and no tears fell. "Rand," saying his name for the first time, she liked the sound of it. "May I ask? I mean this is personal so—"

"Kiley, you can ask me anything."

"Why were you paying someone to have your baby? Why not ... I mean ... marry and..." She broke off looking down. Embarrassment heating her face.

"Have it naturally." He finished for her.

She nodded, raising her head to study him.

"I guess the biggest thing is I don't love any woman right now and didn't want a loveless marriage."

"But why not wait? You're not that old."

"Well, thank you very much." He laughed.

"I didn't mean ..." She blushed again. "I meant that you have plenty of time to be a father."

"Actually, I only have eleven months."

"Eleven months!" Automatically she reached for him trying to see if something was wrong, which looking at him, she couldn't fathom. She had never seen a more virile-looking man.

As if reading her mind, he said. "No, Kiley, nothing's wrong with me." He caught her hand, keeping hold of it. "I'm perfectly healthy. There's no concern of catching anything from me."

He grimaced. "Actually, this isn't going to put me in a very good light, but I want you to know I'll always tell you the truth. So when you're nine months pregnant, and I tell you you're huge, you'll know it's the truth, and if I tell you you're beautiful, it too will be the truth. Okay?"

He waited until she nodded, then letting go of her hands. He rose and moved away to the window. The light shot down on his dark brown hair giving it gold highlights. She watched, her blue eyes intense. He sighed. "The truth is my grandfather conditioned it in his will."

"Will?"

"My grandfather liked to control things. I was his greatest challenge. He wanted me happy and settled down. I don't fault him for that. I know he loved me, but I don't like being manipulated into things. Anyway, the will had a loophole. It said only to produce an heir – nothing about marriage."

"So you found a woman willing to have your baby." Understanding hit her.

"Yes, actually it wasn't as hard as it sounds. The thing is, I'm not against marriage. I'd hope to get married someday. I just hadn't found the right woman. Anyway, my grandfather dangled a carrot in front of me he knew I couldn't resist, though it would serve him right if I did."

"What was it?" she asked then felt embarrassed for prying.

Rand just smiled. "My carrot is Roe Technology. Grandfather started the company. I took over the running of it about ten years ago. He knew what it meant to me and also knew I wouldn't let it go to my step-grandmother and her children."

He gave her a derisive smile. "You'd have to meet them to understand. We don't get along very well, and there's too much at risk letting Roe go to them. Besides, having a child is very appealing to me."

What he said sounded selfish. Except that loneliness and sincerity which, though he tried to hide it with his nonchalant manner, came through loud and clear. There was more to him than selfishness and money, nonetheless Kiley had heard of Roe Technology and knew they were talking about a lot of money.

She wasn't sure how to answer, so said the first thing in her mind. "I guess you got your baby." The instant it was out, she regretted the flippant sound, especially as he jerked.

"Kiley," he turned to her. "I'm sorry this happened to you."

This time she couldn't say anything, afraid she'd cry. At her silence, he continued. "I can't say I'm sorry about the baby. I'm grateful you won't have an abortion. I promise, I'll take care of everything. You don't need to worry."

"I'm okay." A tear trickled down her cheek. "Really, it's just, this is not how I imagined it."

"Sorry about that." Dr. Matthews breezed into the room. "Something came up with one of my other patients. I'm going to have to head over to the hospital. I really hate to leave you like this, but it's an emergency."

"I'm okay now," Kiley assured him.

"You do have some color back in your cheeks. Still, Laura would have my head if I didn't take care of you. This whole situation is just too unbelievable. I feel responsible."

"But you're not." She jumped to his defense.

"Well, I did talk you into the test. And it's a clear case of medical negligence."

"But it wasn't your fault."

"No, it was the ego of Doctor Norman Harvey. Still, we have put you in an awkward position, and I don't like it."

Kiley smiled at the old man's huffing.

"If you need anything at all, even if just to talk, don't hesitate. Or you can call and talk to Laura. I usually don't discuss cases with my wife, but unless you don't want me to, I know she'd be concerned."

"It would be all right to tell her," Kiley said, thinking it might be nice to talk with another woman She had absolutely no idea what to expect, and she like Laura Matthews.

He nodded. "She won't let it get around. You'll have to think what you wish to tell everyone when it becomes noticeable, but there is no concern of that now. This is a prescription for prenatal vitamins. I want you to start taking them immediately. Dolores will give you an information packet on your way out. You're in good health, but I want you to get more rest and try not to overdo it," he said forcefully as he handed her a prescription.

"No heavy lifting or climbing on things. If you have any cramping or pain, I need to know immediately. Otherwise, I won't need to see you for six weeks." He gave her hand a squeeze, then leaned over and kissed her cheek. "Call if you need anything." He waited for her promise before leaving them.

"I will."

ଚ୫ଓ

A few minutes later, Rand had Kiley settled in the soft leather seats of his Lexus, with the information packet the nurse gave them in her lap. They'd hardly pulled out of the parking lot when exhaustion seemed to overtake her. She drifted off to sleep in mid-sentence.

He glanced at her. She was amazing, intriguing and so delightful. He couldn't believe how she'd handled everything. Yes, she'd been overwhelmed, but he'd never forget the way she came up in defense of the baby growing in her – his baby. There was something very special about Kiley Adams.

Pulling up in front of the address she'd given him, Rand turned off the car and took a moment to study the tidy, old rambler painted white with blue trim. Flowers filled the gardens that were spread all around the yard. To one side, next to a small garage, sat a rusted Toyota with more years then he cared to guess. Looking back at the house, he thought simple, fresh, with a touch of old-fashioned elegance. It described both the house and the woman next to him.

"Kiley," he said gently, resisting the urge to run his finger along her cheek. "Kiley, you're home."

She let out a breath, raised her head and blinked several times, looking around. "It wasn't a dream," she said softly.

"At least you didn't say nightmare. It's real."

He reached for her hand. Mindful of the bandages Dolores had put on her scrapes, he squeezed her fingers gently. Heat tingled up his arm. "What happened?" He turned her hand over to look at her palm. "With everything else, I didn't ask."

"I fell."

He could see her self-consciousness as she pulled her hand away, resting it in her lap, interlocking her fingers with those of her other hand. Silently, he waited for her to say more, the tactic worked.

"I was waiting to cross the street. I thought I was pushed, but no one saw it. The police officer figured someone must have bumped into me by accident. I just remember the shove and falling into the street." She shuddered.

A cold chill went down his back at her next words.

"I thought the bus would hit me." Tears trickled down her cheeks.

Rand slid an arm around her shoulder and brushed the tears away with his other hand. "You fell in front of a bus," he restated, the possibility of what could've happened hit him like a blow. She could've been killed. He wanted to wrap her tight, but kept his hold lose, afraid of overwhelming her. "You poor darling. You have had one major shock after another today."

As if realizing she was leaning on him once again, Kiley set back and fumbled with the door handle. "I'm okay. Thank you for giving me a ride home." By the time she got the door open, he was out and made it around the car to help her.

"I'll see you in."

"That's not necessary." She hesitated.

"I think it is. We still have a few things to discuss."

"Wh-what?"

He leaned down and whispered. "Like the baby." Looking around at her neighbor's houses, he continued. "I think it would be better discussed inside."

"But …"

"Come on, Kiley."

She followed helplessly as he led her up the walk to the door. When he reached out for the key, she stepped by him, opening the door herself in an unmistakable show of defiance. Rand tried unsuccessfully to hold back a grin. The more he got to know of her, the more he liked her.

Inside, the furnishings were decidedly old, most antiques, but it was warm, comfortable, with kind-of a country charm, and neat as a pin. Live plants and dried floral arrangements filled the home.

"Very beautiful." He fingered the arrangement sitting on the hall table.

"Thank you. Can I get you something?" she asked, making her way to the kitchen.

"Just water, thank you. Did you do the arrangements?" He remembered Dr. Matthews saying something about it.

"Yes, my grandmother taught me when I was young. When my grandfather died, we did them to support ourselves. I have three boutiques I supply regularly, two others on occasion and I do custom pieces."

"Sounds like you do quite well."

"Not bad, I grow what I can to keep the costs down. And I was able to supplement our income with odd jobs."

"Dr. Matthews indicated your grandmother hasn't been gone long."

She nodded. "Just over two months, she was sick about four years, so though I miss her, I'm glad she's out of pain."

"How long has your grandfather been gone?"

"Almost five years, it was a heart attack, very sudden." She shifted, looking back at him.

"I feel like I am prying, but what about your parents?" he asked.

"They died when I was twelve. It was a stormy night, and they had gone out for the evening. I was spending the night here with my grandparents. A big truck slid going around the curve and rolled. The police said they both died instantly."

"Any other family?"

"Not really. My father's mother died when he was young, and his father remarried when my dad was a teen. They have a couple of other children together. The difference of ages made it so he was never close to the others kids and didn't fit in the family very well. They live in Florida. I went to visit them once when I was in high school. The only other time I ever met them was at my parents' funeral."

She shrugged, but it didn't hide her loneliness. Everything about Kiley said she needed to be loved and to give love. He couldn't have picked out a better mother for his baby.

Putting down her glass, she went to the cupboard above the fridge, and stretched up her arms. Kiley let out a whimper. Rand was out of his chair and by her side, catching the cookie jar before it could slip through her fingers.

"Are you all right?"

She nodded, but she'd gone the pale again. "I'm a little sore."

"Why don't you go lay down on the couch. I'll bring your drink and a couple cookies."

"That's not necessary." Her objection carried little strength.

"I know, but let me do it."

When Rand came out of the kitchen not two minutes later, Kiley was already asleep. He placed the glass on a coaster and the plate of cookies next to it on the table. He then took an afghan from the back of the chair, unfolded it and draped it over her. Unable to stop himself, he brushed back a lock of silken hair from her cheek. *So beautiful.*

As much as he didn't want to leave, he knew Kiley needed her rest. Looking at the time on the mantle-clock confirmed that it was later than he thought.

# Chapter Four

Kiley jerked upright, not sure what had awakened her. She groaned at the stiffness in her body. For a moment, she was unsure where she was. Recognizing her living room, she relaxed, only to jerk up again when the wind tipped over one of the wicker chairs on the front porch. The storm the weatherman had predicted had arrived, but so far no rain was falling.

*The flowers!* The words screamed in her mind.

She groaned again, rising as fast as her aching muscles would allow. She headed for the laundry room. Grabbing her jacket, she didn't stop to pull it on before stepping outside.

The wind tore the door from her grip banging it back against the house. Struggling against the wind made it almost impossible to get her arms in her sleeves. It didn't take long to realize that any attempt at covering the flowers wasn't going to help. The wind was too strong.

She turned back toward the house and caught a glimpse of a man cutting across the front yard. At first, she felt sorry for the man out in the storm, then his furtive movements sent a sharp jolt of fear through her.

Making a dash for the house, she almost slipped on the stairs, but caught the door handle keeping herself upright. Inside, she paused long enough to lock the door of the sun porch, then dash through the back door. Slamming it, she turned the lock and fell back against the wood.

Kiley gulped a couple of breaths before running to the front door. It was already locked. Rand must have done it when he left. When she went to check the windows, she saw the car parked across the street.

Terrified, she pulled back, then peeked around the curtain. The faint light from the streetlamp revealed a man sitting in it. Unfortunately, it wasn't bright enough to see him clearly. Keeping out of sight, she peeked again, then headed for the phone.

Next to the phone in bold handwriting was a note. *I'll call in the morning or you can call me.* There were three phone numbers on the page besides the words, home, office and cell.

She picked up the phone tempted to call Rand Monroe's cellphone, then she realized that the man in the car could've been him checking on her. Dropping the receiver back down, she went to the window and edged back the curtain, peeking out once more. The car was gone and so was any chance of her getting sleep anytime soon.

The couple times she had managed to drift off, she'd been plagued with nightmares of stalking shadows, thunderous buses and running to protect her baby from demons trying to steal it away, all whipped together in raging winds.

At five o'clock she'd given up on all attempts of sleep, changed into jeans and a sweatshirt and got busy on floral arrangements. As soon as it was light enough to see, Kiley braved the wind to check on what damage was done to her gardens. What she found were petals ripped off flowers and broken branches crushing plants. She wanted nothing more than to sink into the rich soil and weep. Instead she headed for the garage and her tools.

It took hours to salvage what blooms she could and prepare them for drying. Then it took several more to try to trim the plants and bushes. It was mid-afternoon before she started to actually clean up the leaves and branches from the yard.

The whole time the wind blew, sometimes buffeting her with powerful gusts, but Kiley kept working, eyeing the heavy, black clouds crossing the horizon. She was just finishing when the first raindrops started. Carrying a load to the garage, she dropped them on the counter, and turned to head back for another load.

"What do you think you're doing?"

Kiley jumped, screeched and would have fallen if Rand hadn't caught her.

"Don't ever do that again." She pulled away from him. Though he stood a full-head taller than her, she felt no fear as she glared up at him. His brown hair was damp, making it appear darker, and she noticed there were gold flecks in his stormy-gray eyes that made them look as if they were burning with their intensity.

"Sorry, but I was getting worried when you didn't answer your phone."

"So you came to scare me to death."

"I apologize for that." He didn't look very apologetic. "Now what do you think you're doing out here?"

"Trying to clean up my garden. What do you think you're doing?" she snapped back.

"Looking for you. I've been calling all day. I probably left a dozen messages on your machine. Don't you ever check your messages?" He left no time for her to answer. "I finally came here because I was afraid something had happened to you, and what do I find? You playing in the rain."

"I'm not playing. I'm working, and I'm just about finished."

"Wrong, you're done now." Grabbing her arm, he headed for the house.

"What are you doing?" She pulled back, but he didn't let go.

"Taking you inside."

"Let me go."

"I don't think so."

"Rand." She dug in her heels.

"Kiley," he objected right back.

"I'm getting mad." Fire filled her eyes.

"I can tell."

"Rand, I mean it, let me go," Kiley said for all the good it did her.

"Not until you're out of the rain," he countered.

"I just need to finish up and put my tools away."

"I'll do it." He continued to the door.

"You're getting your suit wet," she pointed out, stunned.

"Then let me get out of the rain."

"But …"

"Kiley, if I wasn't worried about hurting the baby, I'd put you over my shoulder."

"What about hurting me?"

"I'd put you over my knee," he answered back, looking exasperated. "I have no intention of hurting you, but I do plan on getting you out of the rain."

"Do you always get what you want?" she challenged defiantly.

"Yes." Changing his motion, he suddenly stepped back and scooped her up in his arms.

Kiley screamed and threw her arms around his neck.

"Much better, I should've done this in the first place. Don't say a word." He was through the door before she could offer another objection. He crossed the enclosed sunroom and entered the kitchen before setting her on her feet.

He held her a minute to make sure she was steady. "Are you all right?"

The look she gave him sizzled with fury. "You wrinkled your suit."

Rand looked down and brushed half-heartedly at the water and wrinkles. "My dry cleaner will appreciate you." He looked her up and down. "Why don't you go change into some dry clothes?"

"What gives you the right to order me around?"

"That wasn't an order. That was a suggestion."

"That was a pretty strong suggestion." She tilted her chin up and glared at him.

"Then I apologize. Can I make you something while you change?"

Kiley threw up her arms. "Oh! Let me guess, your middle name is obstinate!"

"Nope, MacArthur."

"You're kidding."

"Afraid not, Randall MacArthur Monroe."

"Maybe I should just call you General," she said partly under her breath.

"Then that would make you a private. So go!"

"This argument is not done," she said over her shoulder in an act of insubordination.

"No arguing among the ranks or I'll give you KP." His lips twitched as if he was having a hard time not letting a smile slip out.

"Sorry, I've decided it's time for some R and R. I'm going to have a hot bath," Kiley said smugly.

"Good, be careful getting in and out."

"I will. Lock the door after you." Kiley stopped long enough to kick off her soaked shoes and left him standing in the middle of the kitchen.

"As you wish," Rand finally let the smile break free as she sauntered away. He'd never had as much fun as he did sparring with her. For a quiet little thing, she sure had a fiery, stubborn streak.

Life was getting fun. He'd never been this playful, but with Kiley it just came naturally, and felt great. Draping his jacket over a chair, he picked up the phonebook and dialed the number to the Chinese restaurant he liked for delivery.

☙❧

The bath felt amazing. Kiley decided it was time to get out when she caught herself dozing off and realized the water had started to chill. She took her time rubbing on her lotion. She'd just pulled on a pair of old, soft lounge pants, when the doorbell rang. For a minute, she debated not going to answer it. Then, with a sigh, she headed down the hall.

Rand was just closing the door when she stepped into the living room. "What are you still doing here?"

"Paying the delivery boy."

"I asked you to lock up after you."

"I did when I came in from putting your tools in the shed." He studied her, liking what he saw. Her hair was piled on her head, little wisps had come free to brush the skin on her neck. Her skin now glowed a soft pink from the warm water.

"That was a hint to leave."

"I know, but Chinese sounded better."

He watched as Kiley took a deep breath, obviously catching the aroma coming from the bags. She couldn't keep back an "Mmm".

Rand grinned, knowing he'd won though she continued to fight it. He waved the bag back and forth. "Wontons, sweet-n-sour pork, shrimp lo mein, cashew chicken and beef broccoli."

"Sold."

"I didn't get anything spicy because I wasn't sure if you liked it or how it would sit," he said as he carried the food into the kitchen with her following.

"Spicy is good, but you're forgiven if you have a fortune cookie in there."

"A whole bag."

"You're forgiven, and I will even let you join me." There was a teasing lilt to her voice as she went to the cupboard and took down two plates.

"That's kind of you."

"If you knew how much I love Chinese food you'd understand."

A few minutes later, Kiley was biting into her second fried wonton when he asked, "If you like spicy, how do you feel about Mexican?"

"I love it, but not too spicy."

"Got it." He made a mental note, filing it away for another date.

"Rand, this is really nice of you. I appreciate it."

"You're welcome."

They fell into a companionable silence broken only by occasional small talk. When they finished eating, they put the leftovers in the fridge and the dishes in the dishwasher then settled in the living room with the bag of fortune cookies.

Kiley cracked open the cookie and slid a piece of the sweet, hard cookie in her mouth. She froze as she stared down at the little slip of paper from the cookie.

"What does it say?" Rand asked at her odd expression.

"The greatest adventure is just starting for you. All dreams are at hand." Kiley had a hard time looking away from the paper. Looking up, she found him watching her. "What does yours say?"

"The best things in life are won with love." He held up another. "Guard your treasures well."

They both fell quiet while opening the next two cookies. "A smile will make a cloudy sky bright," she read. "I'd say today could use quite a few smiles." She looked to him.

"Honor is a blessing to those who hold it. Very profound," Rand commented.

"Uh-huh," She snuggled into the cushion. Her head rested back and heavy eyelids closed.

"You're sleepy." He glanced at his watch. "Early night for you."

She opened her eyes still looking drowsy. "I didn't sleep very well last night." She looked at the darkening sky outside the window. "Rand, when did you leave last night?"

"About fifteen minutes after you fell asleep."

"You didn't come back to check on me?"

"No." He watched her, sensing something more was there. "Kiley, what's wrong?"

"You didn't come back?" she asked again.

He shook his head. "No." When she fell silent Rand tried to wait before he pressed, but his unease got the best of him. "Kiley?"

She looked up at him. Fear showed in her bright blue eyes. "It's ... just someone was watching me last night."

"Someone was in the house." He sat forward, his muscles tightened.

"No, outside. Look, I'm sure it was just my imagination. I had a rough day, and the storm woke me." She tried to shrug it off.

"Tell me all of it." He softened his voice, forcing gentleness in it and Kiley gave in whether because she trusted him, or she was too tired to act as if it was no big deal.

"The storm woke me just before one. I had to cover my flowers so I went out to try, but the wind was blowing too hard. I did what I could, which wasn't very much. I should have cut them before the winds started. Anyway, I was about to head back to the house when I saw someone run across the front lawn. I ran in." When a shiver coursed through her body, he encircled her with his arms. Kiley didn't even seem to realize he had moved to sit beside her, she just leaned into him.

"It frightened you." It wasn't a question, just a gentle soothing statement accompanied with his hand rubbing up and down her back.

She nodded. "The person stayed out front, sitting in a car across the street. I saw him when I was checking the windows."

"You should've called the police."

"And told them about a man sitting in his car."

"Yes, they could have checked him out."

She shrugged.

"You could have called me."

"It was late and …" she broke off.

"You thought it was me," he answered for her.

She nodded again. "I thought you might be checking up on me. You seemed so concerned. I didn't want to embarrass you."

"But, you were frightened. Kiley if that ever happens again, call the police and call me. No matter the time, day or night, I want you to call me." He didn't like the thought of her being in the house alone and afraid.

"I'm sure it was just my imagination. The dark, the storm …" she stared down at her hands. "I was feeling a lot of anxiety. It was giving me nightmares."

He placed a hand under her chin and tilted it up to face him. "If you need me, call! I mean it. It has nothing to do with the baby. It's about your safety."

"All right," she whispered softly.

"Good. Why don't you get some sleep now? I'll stay here tonight."

"Stay. You can't," she pulled back.

"It's all right. I'll sleep on the couch, but I want to be near if you need me."

"But … but, I can't have you stay here. What would people think? It would look like …" Her words petered out.

"Kiley, have you thought what it will be like in a few months. When the pregnancy becomes noticeable. People are going to wonder."

She pulled away, getting up to cross the room. She played with the leaves of a plant.

"Kiley, have you thought of it?"

"I've tried not to."

"Well, I thought of it last night. I thought of how it would affect you, having people think that you got pregnant without getting married. I know in this day and age it's not like it was fifty or even twenty years ago, but it isn't you. You're not comfortable with it. I came up with the logical conclusion. I think we should get married." As soon as Rand said the words, he knew he truly wanted to marry Kiley.

"Married, but you don't love me."

"I don't see that as a problem."

"Well I do. If you wanted to be married, you would have married the other woman who was going to have the baby."

"I didn't want to marry her."

"Rand, I am not going to force you to marry me. I can take care of myself. I've been taking care of my grandmother and myself for years. I inherited the house from her. It's paid for. I just have a little funeral expenses left, and I know how to work to pay for them. And as far as other people, I guess what I know about myself will have to be enough. It's nobody else's concern anyway."

"Kiley —"

"No!" she said firmly. "I don't want a marriage that will end in divorce. I don't want a marriage without love. I want to love my husband, and I want him to love me. I might not have picked to have a baby now, but as long as I can take care of myself and the baby, that is how it will be."

When he started to reply, she held up her hand. "Please, I'm tired. I'd like to go to bed now. Thank you for dinner," she added so properly that Rand smiled.

"You're welcome." He picked up his suit coat off the dining room chair. At the door he paused, looking back at her. "For now I'll leave because I think you do need the rest, and you're hard to handle when you're tired, but I want you to know this isn't through. I want you to think about marrying me."

CR80

Think of marrying him she did. All through the night while the storm raged outside, uncertainty raged within her. She thought of the child he wanted, the one that was developing in her. Thought of what was right. What was fair for him, for her, and for the baby? Rand's controlling, demanding attitude and his concern, his warm smile, and his laughter. The most disturbing thoughts of all were those of his hands on her arm, on her cheek, and of being lifted, carried, and held in his arms.

"I'm not going to fall in love with him," she said aloud, wrapping elastic around a newspaper for her paper route. She was reaching for another newspaper when the phone rang. It took almost five minutes to write up the order for the four-foot swag from the Touch of Home, which was one of her best customers. Fortunately, she had all the flowers she needed for it. She put the phone down promising it there by the next Monday.

The phone hardly made it into the cradle before it rang again. "Good morning." Rand's voice greeted her.

"Actually, it's almost noon."

"I didn't want to wake you, and I wasn't sure about morning sickness. How are you feeling?"

"Good, I was a little queasy when I got up, but that was almost five hours ago. I was just about to grab some lunch. I have left over Chinese."

"Sounds good."

"I thought so."

"Did you sleep well?"

"Yes." She flinched at the first untruth she'd ever told him, but there was no way she was going to tell him that she had stayed awake most of the night thinking of him.

"Please tell me you're not out working in your yard today."

"I'm not. I've been fixing up a swag for a shop that is going to pick it up anytime now. Then I have to deliver my papers."

"Papers?"

"Newspapers."

"You're kidding." Disbelief was evident in his voice even through the phone.

"Nope."

"Don't kids usually deliver newspapers?"

"Yes, but this is just a small, local paper that comes out once a week. I've been delivering it for over two years for a little extra money. Its good exercise and I enjoy getting out. I used to wrap while I talked with my grandmother, then delivered when the home health nurse was here with her for her weekly check and visit."

"It's raining out there."

"That's why I'll wear a jacket."

"Can someone else do it?"

"No, I agreed to do it, and I have to do it because I had to have a replacement last week while I was gone." She could hear his objection coming. "Rand, if you're going to get bossy, I'm going to hang up."

"Kiley."

"I'll talk to you later. I need to do the last touches on the swag and have lunch. Bye."

"Kiley!"

She heard him call her name as she put the phone down.

# Chapter Five

Kiley had to admit this was not her favorite weather for delivering papers. She was only halfway done, and she was already soaked and cold. This was the roughest section – a hill with a cul-de-sac on one side. She'd already done the cul-de-sac. Now she just had the rest of the hill. Fortunately, there was only about an eighth of a mile to the top, then it was a gradual downhill after that.

Kiley moved farther to the side of the road at the sound of a car coming up the hill. Even walking on the opposite side, with this much water on the road, the spray from the tires would drench her. Behind her the powerful engine whined, picking up speed. The noise made her skin crawl. Stepping to the edge of the road, she turned to watch the car pass.

Her first thought was that the guy shouldn't ride the center so much, then she realized he wasn't just hugging the center – he was crossing over, heading directly at her. Reflexes had her throwing her arms up, as if to ward off the car, but the movement saved her instead. The sudden action on the slick pavement combined with the bulky bag, over-balanced her. She fell backward, out of the way, as the car screamed passed. The newspapers cushioned her fall, but Kiley still hit the ground hard, tumbling and sliding several yards down the embankment before coming to a stop.

For the first moment, she was too stunned to move. The next, she hurt too much to. She lay there several minutes to let the pain ease and confusion settle before she tried to shift.

She made it upright to a sitting position, then nausea hit her, but it settled quickly when she dropped her head between her legs. A couple deep breaths and she turned to her knees, shifting the bulky newspaper bag so she could stand. The instant she put weight on her left foot she went down again, holding her ankle as it throbbed mercilessly.

After five minutes had passed and no cars went by, Kiley figured it was up to her to get herself out of the ditch. On hands and knees she made her way up the bank.

"Miss Adams!" A young male voice called out to Kiley. She shifted to watch the boy coming up the hill, water squishing out from under the tires of his bike.

"Danny! Am I glad to see you."

"Are you okay?"

"I fell."

Reaching her, the twelve-year-old boy hopped off the bike and dropped it on the ground.

"Can you help me up?"

He immediately stuck out his hand. Kiley made it up, but still couldn't put any weight on her foot.

Danny knelt down and with great authority announced, "It's already swelling. You probably sprained it. It should be checked to be sure. We should leave the shoe on. If we take it off, you'll never get it back on. Do you have anything to wrap it with?"

"I don't think so, unless my scarf will work."

"That should work. Sit back down." With his help she made it to the ground. "I was pretty good at this when we did it in boy scouts last month," he said as he wrapped it behind the ankle and under the foot.

"Well, I'm sure glad you were here."

"I was looking for you."

"You were?" she said surprised.

"Yeah, there was a man at your house looking for you. He knew about your route so I thought he was okay, but I still didn't tell him where you were. You can't be too careful. You're real pretty."

Kiley smiled at the boy watching after her. "Thank you, Danny. You're right not to tell things to strangers."

Rain flattened his blonde hair to his head but his deep set dimples flashed at her. He was turning into such a great young man. She'd seen him grow up from a baby.

Her thoughts went to the child developing in her. It seemed too impossible to believe. She couldn't help wonder if it would be a boy or girl. If it was a boy and had her hair he might look something like Danny when he was older. The picture that formed in her head was of a tall, lean boy with darker hair who looked much like his father.

"He said so, too. But I think he was still mad."

Her attention snapped back to the present and the boy standing beside her. "Was he driving a red sports car?" she asked, and glanced in the direction the car that almost hit her had disappeared.

"Nope. Maybe I should ride home and get my mom to pick you up."

Of course it wouldn't be the same car. She was being paranoid. She shoved the thought away and turned her attention back to the boy. "Let's see first how I do standing now?"

"Maybe it would be better if you took off the newspaper bag."

"You're probably right."

He helped her work the cumbersome bag over her head.

Once again, with his help, she made it up. This time though, with Danny's wrap, she could put a little weight on it, but there was no way she could walk.

"I think I better get my mom."

Before Kiley could answer, they heard another car coming up the hill. There was a moment of fear then relief and strange excitement when she caught sight of the familiar white car.

"That's the guy that was asking about you." The awe in the boy's voice was unmistakable.

The car slammed to a stop in the middle of the road just a couple of feet from the pair. Rand got out of the car, wearing a dark suit, raincoat and a very serious expression. To say he looked powerful was an understatement.

"Hi." She tried to say it cheerfully, but from the dark look he gave her, she knew he wasn't happy.

"What happened? You're soaked and covered with mud."

Evident that the man knew Kiley, Danny spoke up before she could muster the words. "She fell and hurt her ankle. I think it's sprained."

Rand's eyes went immediately to her foot. Kiley was glad she hadn't mentioned the red car had almost hit her.

"Let's get you into the car," Rand said, reaching for her arm.

"My newspapers." She pointed to the ground.

"You first, then we'll worry about those blasted papers."

Kiley looked at him and realized that he was barely holding his anger in. "But I agreed to deliver them."

"I can do them, Kiley," Danny volunteered.

"You can do them for her?" Rand turned to the boy.

"Sure, I know her whole route. I sub for her whenever she needs."

"Good man. I'll tell you what. I'll give you twenty bucks for finishing the papers today."

The boy looked about to burst at the prospect but answered, "You don't need to pay me. I'd do it for Miss Adams."

"A deal's a deal," Rand came back, "And, how about I give you another hundred to do the route the rest of the month and next month. After that the route's yours if you want it. Kiley's quitting." When she started to object, he sent a glare her way.

The boy's mouth dropped open, but he couldn't get a word out.

"Is it a deal?" Rand asked, sticking out his hand.

"You bet." Finding his voice, Danny shook Rand's hand.

"Great. First, let's get Kiley in the car."

"But I'm all filthy." This time she got the protest out, not that it had anymore effect on him.

"I noticed." He took her arm for support, and Danny took her other side.

"I'll ruin your interior."

"I don't care about the interior." A little of his control slipped.

"Don't you at least have a blanket?"

Rand glanced toward heaven as the rain came down on them. Kiley guessed he wasn't praying for the rain to stop.

"All right," he conceded. "I've got a blanket in the trunk." Seconds later, he wrapped the blanket around her and helped her into the car. He then pulled out his wallet and handed the boy a hundred and twenty dollars. "Don't lose it."

"No, sir." Danny put it in his jacket pocket and zipped it up. "You'll take care of Miss Adams?"

"I will," Rand promised, handing the youth the newspaper bag.

Danny waved to her and headed up the hill on his bike as Rand came around the car.

"You've got quite a champion there," he commented as he settled in the car, heading for the hospital. "You know he has a crush on you."

"Yes, and that was rotten, and you know it."

"What was rotten? Wasn't I fair?"

"You know what I mean. Giving him that money, knowing I couldn't say anything because it meant so much to him. That was sneaky and you know it."

"You're right, but you shouldn't be out in this weather, and certainly shouldn't be carrying that heavy bag. Dr. Matthews said no heavy lifting. How many papers did you have in there anyway?"

Knowing it was no use, she answered. "About fifty. I have a hundred and fifty-four, but I split the route in half. I'd done the first and had almost finished half of the second."

When Rand didn't say another word, Kiley figured he was back to praying for patience. He was silent for quite a while. Coming to a stop at a red light, he reached out his hand, touched and tilted up her chin. "You scratched your cheek." There was an odd softness in his voice. "What happened?"

"I fell."

"How?"

"A car was coming up the road. I stepped back out of the way." If he hadn't have been looking so intently at her, he might have missed the shiver she couldn't keep in.

"Tell me."

"I thought it was going to hit me. He crossed the road and came right at me."

Kiley couldn't make out what he muttered, as he took off when the light changed, and figured it was for the best. She was also relieved when he let it drop but doubted it was the end of it. Still, it was a much needed reprieve. She snuggled down in the blanket.

Fifteen minutes later, Kiley started to protest when they pulled up to the hospital. "Rand, I don't need to be here for a sprained ankle. Couldn't we just go to Dr. Matthews' office and have him look at it."

"No, it needs to be x-rayed."

"But."

"You're a very sensible person. Why are you arguing?"

She was silent for a moment. "Because my medical insurance isn't very good. There's a high deductible when it comes to emergency room visits. I can't afford it, especially without my paper route money."

"Don't worry about it. You're covered."

"Rand, you can't just pay things for me."

"Yes, I can. Besides, you have very good insurance coverage. It'll cover all but the twenty-five dollar deductible."

"What do you mean?" She looked at him suspiciously.

"You're on my policy as of three days ago, as my significant other."

"How?"

"Easy. All I needed was your social security number and date of birth."

"But you don't … how did you get my social security number." Her irritation was tempered by her surprise and curiosity.

"It really isn't hard to find out all you need to know about a person if you know where to look, or have a connection to those who do. You know, you really surprised me that you only have one credit card and nothing on it. That's impressive."

"It's only for emergencies. My grandmother didn't like them. She said they encouraged spending money that wasn't yours."

"I wish I could have met your grandmother."

"You would have liked her. She was the ultimate grandmother. Grandpa was great, too. He used to play ball with me. I was his little sweetheart."

"I can believe that." Rand kept her talking as much to find out about her as to keep her mind off her ankle. In spite of the tragedy of losing her parents at such an early age, Kiley had a remarkably good youth. She got so caught up in sharing her life with him that she forgot about his underhandedness in obtaining information on her for the insurance.

Three hours later, when they pulled into her driveway, Kiley sported a wrapped ankle and a pair of crutches, which Rand had picked up at the pharmacy along with her prenatal vitamins.

"No," she objected when he went to lift her out of the car. "I can make it. You don't need to carry me." Resolute, he opened the trunk and drew out an umbrella, before retrieving her crutches from the back seat.

She was leaning against the car when he turned back to her. "Thank you," she said, taking the crutches as he held the umbrella over her. Awkwardly, she made her way to the house on her own. Despite the umbrella, what drying her clothes had done at the hospital, she was soaked once more by the time they made it inside.

"It would've been faster if I'd have carried you." Rand complained, hanging up her wet jacket on the hall tree, before taking off his own and placing it beside hers.

"I need to learn to maneuver on these things."

"Yeah, but you don't need to do your practicing in the rain. Why didn't you wear a heavier jacket? You're freezing."

"With the bag on and walking, I bake and it's usually enough to keep me dry."

"Well, let's get you dry and warmed up. Do you have any cocoa?"

"Of course." She gave him a mysterious little smile.

"Okay." He wondered what was up. "I'll put on some water while you change."

"The tea kettle is on the bottom shelf, left of the stove."

He had the water on when he heard his name called. Cautiously, he moved down the hall. The first room was a bedroom full of beautiful antiques, across the hall was a sewing-storage room, which was neat and tidy. Kiley called him again and he followed it to the room at the end of the hall where the door was closed.

"Kiley," he paused outside it.

"In here, you can open the door."

He found her sitting on the bed with a forlorn look. The room was feminine, but not uncomfortably so, with a hunter and rose floral spread and matching curtains.

"Will you go to the next room, on the floor by the chair is a large sewing basket."

It took him a second to take his eyes off her before he could move to the sewing room. She was in the same position when he returned with the basket and placed it beside her.

She blushed deeply. "I can't get my pants off." She nodded to the large wrap on her foot.

In the kitchen, the teakettle whistled.

"I'll be right back." Rand dashed out of the room. The water wasn't the only thing steaming. She looked so appealing sitting there on her bed. And when she blushed, Rand knew he was in trouble. There was no question about it. He wanted Kiley and not just in his or her bed. She was not that kind of girl. She was the forever kind, and that was how he wanted her – forever. Now the question was just how to go about it. She didn't take his previous proposal very serious.

Coming back down the hall, he found her awkwardly trying to open the side seam of her pants. From the gasp she made, she was causing herself a great deal of pain.

"Here," he took the seam ripper from her hand and dropped it in the basket, taking out the scissors.

"What? No! Rand. I know they're old and worn but I was trying to save ..." she said as he cut through the hem up her leg, "them."

"They're not worth hurting yourself." Unmindful of his suit, he squatted in front of her, rested her foot on his thigh, then he proceeded to cut the seam up her leg. "All right, Kiley, undo your pants."

"What?" she squeaked out.

"I'll help you get them off."

"I can do it myself."

"Be reasonable. You can't stand. You can't balance. Just to move hurts you. I'm not going to jump your bones, though the thought does have a great amount of appeal."

Her bottom lip was caught between her teeth but she made no move.

"Look," he rose going to the closet, took out her robe then came back to crouch in front of her. "Put this across your lap." When she still didn't move, he started again. "Do you have a tattoo or something on that cute little derriere you're trying to hide?"

"Funny," she finally answered, spreading the robe over her lap then reached underneath to undo her pants. She gasped as Rand put his hand under the robe and pulled her pants down.

"Just think of me as your doctor."

"Not hardly."

He smiled. "Don't you just love wet denim?" His hands brushed the inside of her knee and he lost his concentration.

"I've never seen you wear jeans." Her comment took him by surprise and helped pull his thoughts back to a safer level. It seemed like he had known her for a long time, not just a couple of days.

"You just always see me right after work. Tomorrow I'll bring Mexican and wear jeans."

"Tomorrow?"

"I'm making a date Kiley. Say yes. I'll see you about six-thirty, so I can have time to go home and change. What kind of movie would you like?" He could see her objection rising, so before she could get it out he said, "Please." He reached out and brushed back a lock of her honey-gold hair, looking deep into her soft blue eyes.

"Yes." Her reply was breathless, like he felt. "But you pick the movie, just no war."

"Adventure or comedy?"

"Either."

"I'll start the water for you. Can you make it to your bath on your own?"

"Yes." She blushed.

"All right, I'll have hot chocolate and sandwiches ready when you come out."

"Hot chocolate is on the top shelf of the pantry. I'd like mint please."

"Mint?"

She nodded.

Rand closed the door and waited outside for her to settle in the tub before he headed for the kitchen. He was crossing the family room when there was a knock at the door. Opening it, he found Danny. The boy carried a small casserole dish and shifted from side to side.

"Hi there, Danny. Come on in."

"Hi, I saw your car and knew you were back. How's Kiley?"

Rand didn't miss the boy calling her by her first name. "You were right. She has a bad sprain and has to be on crutches for a week."

The boy nodded, clearly pleased at being given recognition. "I told my mom what happened. She sent this casserole over." He held up a towel wrapped dish that emitted a wonderful aroma of herbs and chicken.

"That was nice of her. Why don't we take it into the kitchen?"

"Where's Kiley?"

"In the bath, I was just making hot chocolate for her when she gets out. Would you like a cup?"

"Sure." He followed Rand in the kitchen. "I'd like the nut kind."

"What is she, some kind of a hot chocolate connoisseur?" he said more to himself but Danny answered.

"No, she just really likes it." Obviously the boy had been treated to it before, as he went to the panty to get the chocolate. Rand picked Hazelnut like the boy.

"I didn't even know they made Raspberry," Rand commented looking at the shelf.

"Yeah, I don't like it. Kiley mainly keeps it for Mrs. Owens. She's older and lives two doors down. Are you Kiley's boyfriend?" The question was straightforward.

If Rand hadn't liked the kid before, he did now. Kiley had a real champion.

"Yes." Fudging a bit, but decided it was for the best.

"Kiley doesn't date much."

"Don't worry. I'll be good to her."

Danny looked thoughtful. "You were a little gruff with her earlier, but you were gentle."

"I was worried."

He nodded, accepting the answer.

"Maybe you can help me, Danny. Did you notice a red car around the time of Kiley's accident?"

Danny shook his head. "Kiley mentioned it, too, but I didn't see it. Is something wrong?"

"It almost hit her. That's how she fell."

"I didn't see anything, but I'll keep watch."

"I'd appreciate that. Just be careful. I don't want you hurt, either."

After the boy promised, the talk switched to sports. They were still talking when Kiley came down the hall, moving awkwardly on the crutches. "Hi, Danny."

"Hi, Miss Adams," she gave a slight frown and he added, "Kiley," softly. "My mom sent over a casserole. I'll pick the dish up tomorrow so you don't have to worry about it."

"That's so nice. Tell your mom thank you for me. And thank you for finishing my route and especially for taking care of me. The doctor said you wrapped my ankle perfectly."

The young man beamed under the praise. Rand could understand his crush on Kiley. He felt the same way. She had a way of making everyone feel special.

Danny drank his hot chocolate and talked for the next twenty minutes before he left. Rand saw him to the door and turned back in time to see Kiley making her way into the family room. She didn't object when he helped her settle on the couch in front of the TV.

She seemed a little surprised when he served her the casserole there. After they finished eating, he took the dishes into the kitchen then retrieved his briefcase from the car. They settled in a companionable silence as he worked on papers. When she rested her head back and closed her eyes, Rand put down his book.

"I think it's time I go and let you get to bed."

"Oh," Kiley looked up and yawned. "Sorry."

"Don't be. Would you like me to help you to your room?"

"I can manage. Do you realize that since you have known me, all you've done is send me to bed and leave?"

"That has been the recurring theme." Then he gave her a wicked grin. "We could always change that to me sending you to bed and my staying."

"I don't think so." She blushed, stumbling over the words.

"I know, but you make it awful tempting."

Kiley just shook her head, than did something that took him by surprise. She leaned over and lightly kissed his cheek. If he were Danny, he wouldn't ever have washed that cheek again. Being Randall Monroe, he slid one hand into her honey wheat hair, keeping her head still while he slowly brought his lips down to brush against hers before they settled firmly.

He felt the jolt of excitement as she returned his kiss. Wishing he could continue forever, instead, he broke the kiss, brushed her lips once more with his then lightly kissed the end of her nose.

"I better go." The words came out husky, but if the brightness of her eyes was any indication, she was just as affected as he had been. He pulled on his raincoat, paused, and then came back to her. "Here." He handed her a cellphone.

"Your phone?" She looked up at him confused.

"No, that is your phone. I've already programmed my numbers into it and Dr. Matthews's. You'll have to put in the others."

"You got me a cellphone?"

"Yes. Keep it with you." He stopped at the door. "Will you be all right?"

"Yes."

"I'll see you tomorrow evening. Call if you need anything."

He left before she could think of any objection about the phone. Not that she really had anything to object to, and decided she really didn't want to argue with him about it.

As soon as the door closed she stood, and made sure the door was locked before heading off to bed.

❀

The next evening, Kiley thought everything was a bit too perfect from Rand's choice in Mexican to the movie he picked – a classic comedy, Bringing Up Baby. The baby that Cary Grant and Audrey Hepburn were trying to handle was a leopard.

Together they laughed at the hilarious antics of the movie. Rand was the same in jeans as he had been in the power suits, though, Kiley knew she hadn't seen the true business side of him. He was a busy man, but didn't seem to let it plague him.

When she questioned him about it, he answered simply. "I still follow the first rule my grandfather taught me. You find good people and let them do their jobs, and then you just have to keep an eye on them and let them know what you expect."

He picked up her hand, running his thumb over her knuckles. Warmth filled her as she looked into his eyes.

"You know," he started, "I didn't think about this when I picked the movie, but they knew each other just a couple of days before deciding to get married. Even with all the crazy things happening to them." He paused. "Kiley, will you marry me?"

Kiley felt her heart lurch. It hit her that more than anything, she wanted to say yes. She could feel the reply slipping out before the logical part of her mind took control. "Rand, it wouldn't be right."

"I think it would be," he returned.

"No."

He sighed and blew out a breath. "Why can't you be like Audrey Hepburn and say 'Yes, David', but make it 'Yes, Rand'."

"Because you're not Cary Grant."

"I'm serious."

"I know, but the answer is still no."

"Kiley, you're going to have my baby. I want the baby to have my name. I want you to have my name."

"No," she said before he could say anymore.

"What if I told you I love you?"

Her heart seized with all her wishes and desires. Unable to stop it, her chin quivered, and her eyes grew watery, but she shook her head.

"Kiley, we should get married now."

She shook her head again. "No." The word was weak.

"It will be better for you. You won't be pregnant without a husband. I'll take care of you." He sounded desperate. "I want you."

"And you always get what you want," she challenged him.

"Are you always so hard-headed?"

"Only around you. Are you always so domineering?"

"Only around you," he countered back.

"Liar."

"I ought to take you over my knee."

"Try it."

Rand let out a very frustrated roar. But Kiley met him straight on. "You won't hurt me and you know it. You're all huff."

"Huff." His fury flared as he swooped down on her. "Let's see about that." His mouth descended on hers forcefully, demanding. Kiley's mouth had O'd, which left her open for the probing of his tongue, sweeping in with tantalizing strokes. Kiley had never known anything so erotic. She felt no fear, knowing at any protest he'd stop, but the taste and feel of him was so incredible she couldn't form a protest.

At the first signs of her surrender, the kiss became gentle and then turned into a hot, loving caress that left her trembling with longing. His hands moved over her back urging her closer. On their own accord, her hands slid up his arms and around his neck, arranging her body in tight alignment, taking in a pleasure she never felt the desire to reach for.

Rand let the kiss go on and on. He was tempted to press it farther, but he knew he had to wait with Kiley. There was such innocence in her actions, he didn't want to scare her or have her pull back from the tender bond he felt developing.

Kiley was too precious to risk losing, and though he wanted her now, he wanted more. He wanted her love, and he wanted marriage, and a lifetime to enjoy the feelings she raised in him. The kiss had more than proved his point that they should be together.

Gradually he released her, feeling the great loss of her being out of his arms. She moved as unsteady as he felt. He felt a rush of satisfaction that she felt just as he had. "Point made." The instant he realized he said the words out loud, he knew he'd made a mistake. Her body stiffened, fire filled her eyes.

"Please, leave." The words held a harshness he'd never heard come out of her mouth before.

"Kiley."

"Go!" she demanded, reaching down for the crutches, struggling to stand.

"Kiley, please."

"Just leave." Turning away, she refused to look at him. When he stepped toward her she turned toward the hall. Falling in her haste to get away from him, she landed against the wall.

Rand started after her, but she steadied herself and made it through the doorway into her room before he could reach her. She slammed the door shut firmly.

He stood in the hallway, hands out, unable to catch back what had in just a few short days become the most important thing in his life. He let out a groan and shoved his hands up through his hair. He had blown it big time.

Rand paced back and forth across the room, until it became evident Kiley wasn't going to come out. He contemplated breaking down the door. Luckily, his common sense finally kicked in and he realized Kiley probably wouldn't see it as a good thing.

Checking the lock on the back door, he grabbed his jacket from the hall tree. He went out. Setting the lock on the door, he closed it then checked to make sure it'd caught behind him. At the car, he stopped to put on his jacket, turning back toward Kiley's house.

*Why did she have to be such a stubborn, independent little thing? She was driving him crazy.*

# Chapter Six

Kiley leaned back against the door, half praying that Rand would come after her. When she finally heard the front door close, she hobbled forward dropping the crutches as she flung herself on the bed, sobbing into the comforter.

*Why did I have to fall in love with him? Why did he have to ask me to marry him? Say he loved me when he didn't?* She cried on and on wishing she could believe his words were true.

Finally, she wondered why she couldn't just pretend they were in love, and marry him. Her love could be enough for both of them, and with the baby, surely she could make it work. Rand would cherish her, look after her just like he had the last couple days. Even if it was for the sake of the baby, he'd been wonderful.

They had a good time together. She'd never known such a good time. There hadn't been any uneasy moments. Even when he bossed her around, there had been something a little bit fun about it and comforting.

She started to cry again, this time wanting him back. She had been unreasonable. He'd be upset with her. Wiping her eyes on the quilt, she eyed the telephone debating if she dared call. For several minutes, she vacillated back and forth, then decided faint hearts never won. She picked up the phone and punched in his number from the card that sat on the nightstand.

On the first ring her confidence dropped, on the second she almost put down the phone. By the third, she was desperate. On the forth, the answering machine kicked on. At the sound of his voice, she began to cry again. At the beep the words rushed out of her. "Rand, I'm sorry." Sobbing too much to continue, she hung up.

Burying her face in her arms, she sobbed harder. She wondered what Rand would think if he was there listening to her message, – worse – what if he wasn't there at all. What if he had gone to another woman? She didn't want to think of that possibility, but couldn't get it out of her mind.

Groggy, she lifted her head. She must have fallen asleep. The dark room was hazy. It took a moment for her sluggish mind to comprehend the smoke around her and then she erupted into a coughing spell.

*Fire!* She choked and coughed, pushing herself up from the bed. Forgetting until the moment her injured foot hit the floor about her ankle, Kiley crumbled in nauseating pain that had her sucking in a lung full of smoke, which caused her to coughed to try to get it back out. Tears flooded her eyes from smoke and pain. The breath she took to clear her head backfired, as again it was all smoke.

Her head swam as she crawled to the door. Instructing herself to remain calm, she bumped into the dresser then reached for the door handle. It wasn't hot, but when she tried to turn it, it failed to open. The knob turned, but no matter how she tugged, she couldn't get it to budge.

In frustration, she slammed her hand against the door, this time she felt heat coming through. She scooted back then turned and crawled for the small side windows which as normal, she left open a crack. She was halfway across the floor when flames shot up from outside and caught ahold of the curtains.

Instantly, the wall ignited. Scrambling back, she went down. Her body was unresponsive as Kiley tried to pull herself up to the bed. She made it halfway to the bed when her strength gave out totally and she slumped to the floor. With her last conscious breath, she sobbed Rand's name, knowing she was never going to get to have his baby, or even tell him she loved him.

ॐ

Too worked up to stop, Rand drove past his house following the winding country road away from the city. If the night would have been clear, he could have seen millions of stars, but just like his relationship with Kiley, too many obstacles blocked them.

Wind and rain rocked the car, forcing his attention to the storm outside. Then it hit him. Maybe he needed to give Kiley his attention. To listen to her before he lost her.

Turning the car around, he headed back to her house. Glancing at the clock, it showed twelve-thirty and he was at least an hour away. His first thought was that he would have to wait until morning but he knew he couldn't. They had to work this out now, whether it was the middle of the night or not. He could not go the night with Kiley mad at him.

All the houses were dark as he drove through her neighborhood until he pulled up in front of Kiley's. Lights flickered around the side of the house. It wasn't until he had stepped out of the car and caught the whiff of smoke that it occurred to Rand the light was not right.

Fear hit him, as in a flash of light, flames leapt up the side of the house. Rand burst in to a run, at the same time pulling his cell phone from his pocket and dialing the emergency number. As soon as the voice answered on the other end, he yelled there was a fire and Kiley's address. He repeated the whole thing then dropped the phone, leaping up the steps.

Throwing his weight against the door, it took three hits before the door burst open. Smoke clouded the room. Flames crackled at the end of the hall, blocking the way to Kiley's room. Still, he started forward.

"Kiley!" he yelled, choking as the smoke entered his lungs. "Kiley!"

The heat forced him back to the entry. Cool air entered through the open door, but did nothing to clear away the smoke from the room. Rand rushed back outside. Not stopping to drink in the blessed freshness, he ran around to the large window of Kiley's room.

He could see the fire raging up the side of the house, but in the front of the house, the larger window was still clear. He could hear the sirens in the distance, but couldn't wait for them to get there. He had to get to Kiley. Grabbing a large stepping stone that ornamented Kiley's garden, Rand threw it through the window.

Sharp edges of glass bit into his arm and hand as he knocked away the glass around the window. He didn't slow as he hoisted himself in. Through the thick smoke he saw Kiley, lying unmoving by the end of the bed. Only eight feet away from where she lay, fire bit at the wall around the smaller side window.

He could feel the heat on his face as he reached for her, pulling her up in his arms. He didn't stop to check if she was breathing, but the groan that escaped her body was reassuring. Smoke choked the air from his lungs. He staggered under the weight of her body. The distance to the window he had covered in three steps before, now seemed like miles.

He staggered again, almost going down. Struggling the last few feet to the window, Rand had to take several deep breaths before his head cleared enough to lower Kiley out the window. He was trying to watch the glass, but the heat at his back urged him to hurry. He was about to let her go when she was lifted from his arms. Rand leapt from the window, rolling as he hit the ground. Behind him, two firemen shot water into the room. Another fireman helped him to his feet.

"Is anyone else in the house?" the fireman asked, getting his attention.

Rand shook his head and coughed trying to get the "no" out, but it was choked into another cough. It didn't matter, the firemen had his answer, and pulled him halfway across the yard before Rand was able to find his voice. "Kiley."

"She's with the paramedics now." The fireman pointed across the street.

Rand followed the motion and saw the cluster of people on the curb. He broke free from the fireman's hold and made it to a half run. Terror filled him when he was close enough to see her still body lying on the soaked, cold ground. Drops of fine misty rain landed on the oxygen mask strapped to her face. One paramedic was taking her blood pressure while the other talked on the radio.

"Kiley." His world tilted and the fireman who had followed him caught his arm, holding him back. 'Kiley." He pulled toward her, but only made it a few feet before he was pushed down on the curb.

"They're taking care of her." The fireman assured him.

As soon as the fireman's attention was diverted, Rand crawled closer to Kiley, careful to stay out of the paramedic's way. Stretching out his hand, he caught a strand of golden hair, running it through his fingers. The tears that stung his eyes were not only from smoke.

One of the paramedics caught his arm, rotating it toward him. "I think we've found the source of the blood." It was the first time Rand noticed the blood that soaked his sleeve, but he didn't care. He only wanted Kiley. The paramedic shifted to cut back his sleeve.

"No, take care of Kiley." Rand tried to pull away, breaking into another coughing spasm.

"Your wife is doing fine," they assured him, trying to press an oxygen mask to his face.

"Please, she's pregnant and has a sprained ankle."

"How far along?" The paramedic added the information to her chart.

"Two weeks."

"You're certain?" There was surprise in the man's voice.

"Yes."

"There should be no danger to the embryo. The only concern will be stress and medications. She's still unconscious but her responses are good. I would say the prognosis is good. Now, will you please put on the oxygen mask? You are both fortunate."

Rand's eyes moved across the street to Kiley's house and wasn't sure she would feel lucky. The damaged was done, though flames no longer ate at it. Firemen milled around the house, some dragging hoses away while others carried axes looking for hot spots. To look at one side of the house, it looked perfectly normal, except for the flashing red lights reflected in the windows. He shuddered at the sight of the other half. There was little left of the corner where Kiley's room had been. Agony raced within. He'd come too close to losing her tonight.

The need to take care of Kiley intensified at an alarming rate. Turning his attention back to her, she was too still. He wanted to snatch her up in his arms and make everything all right. He had grown up with a privileged life, having most anything he wanted. It was only luck that he found pleasure in working for what he desired.

Even in business nothing was ever kept from him when he went after it. Now, for the first time in his life, he was unsure if he could obtain his goal, which was making Kiley his. He faced the reality that nothing he would ever have would be as precious.

CARD

Light was the first thing that registered when Kiley opened her eyes. The next was the burning in her lungs and eyes, which brought back the memories of the fire. Smoke permeated every breath she took. Still, she could make out the nauseating antiseptic smell of a hospital.

"Kiley," she turned to the hoarse voice hardly recognizing it as Rand's. "Hi, sweetheart."

"Rand," she choked out.

"Shh, your throat is irritated." He took a deep breath. "The smoke."

Soot streaked his face and clothes. His hair looked as if it hadn't been combed for a month. He had never looked such a mess, and he had never looked so good.

"The fire."

"Shh." He caught her hand bringing it to his lips. White gauze was wrapped around his one hand and forearm.

"You're hurt."

"It's nothing." He kissed her fingers.

"You got me out, you … came back."

"I couldn't leave with discord between us."

She opened her hand against his cheek. "Is the … baby?"

"They said there is nothing to be worried about. You had me worried when you didn't wake up. You also didn't do your ankle any good. They said you tried to stand on it. The main concern is your lungs with all the smoke you breathed in. They're going to move you upstairs for the night."

"Can't I go … my home!" Tears filled her eyes.

Rand leaned down wrapping his arms around her, pressing her head into his neck. "Shh, sweetheart, what's important is that you're all right. They will save what they can."

"But where will I go, what will I do?"

"Shh, you have my house."

"But –"

"No, you will stay with me."

"We're not –"

He cut her off again. "We will be as soon as you're strong enough." He could see her objection coming. "Please, I almost lost you. Tell me I'm selfish, manipulative, anything. I'll admit it, but please, say you will marry me. I need you with me. Please! No pressures. I promise. I just need you safe."

"Rand." A lone tear trickled down her cheek. He cared for her. At least she was certain of that. The yes was on her lips, but she didn't get it out before the doctor entered the cubicle.

"You're awake. I wasn't told. How do you feel?" He already had his stethoscope out and up to her chest.

"Tired, and my throat hurts."

"Heaviness in breathing?"

"A little."

"Well, the lungs sound good, but you did lose consciousness for over an hour. They're on their way to move you upstairs so we can monitor you through the night. If all looks fine, we'll release you around noon."

"My baby?" She couldn't help asking.

He nodded. "I was informed, but everything looks okay. Though, I want you to get plenty of rest."

The doctor left as the nurse and attendant came in to move her. With all the shuffling, Kiley still didn't get to answer Rand.

Once settled on the third floor, she waited for him to come. It was nearly four o'clock in the morning. She found it hard to keep her eyes open. The pill they gave her, after assuring her it wouldn't harm the baby, was making her drossy. She fought to stay awake, but it was rapidly becoming a losing battle. Finally, her eyelids drifted down.

She was almost asleep when she felt Rand's lips brush across her cheek. Forcing her eyes half open. "Rand." His name was heavy on her lips.

"Go to sleep, darling." His finger brushed her cheek in a gentle caress. If she didn't know she loved him before, she knew it at that moment. She just hoped it would be enough for them both.

"Rand, I have to … tell you. " Her words came out slurred. "Yes."

"Yes?"

"I want to marry …," her words petered out. Her eyes wouldn't stay open any longer. Sleep conquered her body.

Rand wanted her back awake to make sure she meant what he thought she did. He wanted to kiss her and tell her he loved her. Then again why not tell her. Brushing his lips against hers, he said the words softly, hoping somehow she heard him. "I love you." He pulled the blanket up tighter. She didn't even stir.

Rand didn't want to leave her but he figured it was his best chance to get cleaned up. He would be back before she woke. Rand crossed the room, at the door he paused and looked back one more time at the woman he had come to love in just a few days.

It was truly amazing how life turned out. With difficulty he forced himself to turn away and move through the door. Carefully, he closed the door behind him, conscious of the slight click it made. With a sigh, he turned and met a man striding toward Kiley's room.

"Wait a minute, you can't go in there." Rand stepped in front of him, blocking the entrance.

"Excuse me?" The man stood almost Rand's height and was a good ten years older.

"You have the wrong room," Rand informed him.

"Kiley Adams?" A gaze was directed at him.

"Yes, but she's asleep. If it is about the insurance, she can talk to you later. She had a bad night and needs rest."

The man pulled a small notebook from his pocket. "You would be Randall Monroe."

"Yes."

"You pulled Miss Adams from her house."

"Yes, look if you're a reporter I really don't want to talk to you right now, and want you to leave Miss Adams alone."

"Pardon me, I'm Detective Paul Gerome." He pulled his badge out, holding it for Rand to inspect.

After a second, Rand nodded to the police officer, sticking his hand out to shake. "Nice to meet you, Detective. Sorry, it's been a long day and a very stressful night. Do you mind if we talk after I get something to drink?"

"Not at all, there's a vending machine in the waiting room." He motioned down the hall, falling into step beside him.

Rand picked a fruit juice while the detective got cola.

"Now, if I might ask. What were you doing at Miss Adams' house at one-thirty in the morning?"

"I needed to talk to Kiley, Miss Adams."

"Do you always go to talk in the middle of the night?"

"No." Rand found himself taking offense to the man's comment.

"What is your relationship with Miss Adams?"

"She's my fiancée."

"So it is common for you to go over at night."

"No, we're not sleeping together. Kiley is very old-fashioned."

Gerome raised an eyebrow. "Then can you tell me why you were there?"

Rand sighed, "Kiley and I had an argument before I left this evening. I drove around and knew I couldn't go to bed until it was resolved between us. So I went back."

"And saw the house on fire."

"Yeah," he shuddered at the thought of how close the flames had been to Kiley.

"You called the fire department."

"I grabbed my cell phone and dialed 911."

"Then what?"

"I kicked in the front door, but the hall was in flames. I couldn't get through, so I ran to her window and broke it out with a rock. The other side window was on fire. Kiley was unconscious. The fireman was there when I lowered her out."

"You cut your arm." The detective nodded to his arm.

"It'll be all right."

"So you'd truly walk through fire for her," he said with mirth.

"Kiley's worth it, beside it's my fault." The guilt he had been feeling rose again.

"Your fault?" the officer asked.

Rand nodded. "I should have checked the fireplace before I left. The screen was up but …"

"The fire didn't start at the fireplace." Gerome said. "Can you tell me, does Miss Adams have any enemies?"

"Kiley?" he said. "Why?"

"Because someone tried to murder Miss Adams last night."

Rand stared in disbelief. "That's impossible."

"I'm afraid not. There is still more investigation to do at the sight, but preliminary evidence shows there were two fires. One started in the hall, the other outside, below her side window."

Rand shook his head. "Nobody could want to hurt Kiley. Wait until you meet her. I didn't even believe there were women like her. She's beautiful, sweet, with a gentle heart. She takes time for neighborhood boys that have crushes on her for heaven's sake. She has spirit, and this determination that you have to love though she has you so exasperated."

Rand realized he was going on and stopped. He ran his fingers back through his hair. "No, no one would want to hurt Kiley." He refused to accept the possibility.

"Mr. Monroe, besides the evidence of dual fires, there are traces of a rope tied to her bedroom door knob and the knob across the hall so she could not open her door. The back door had been forced. The guy was definitely not a professional. The door also wasn't closed when he left." Gerome looked directly at him. "Kiley Adams would have died in that house if you hadn't shown up when you did."

Rand was too numb to say anything. The detective gave him a moment before he continued on to the next question. "What about the boy with a crush?"

"Boy, oh no it couldn't be, he's just a kid."

"Could he be upset enough with her getting engaged?"

"No, I'm serious. He's just a kid about twelve. And he kind of gave me his blessing. It was really something, he was so protective of her when …," Rand's words died in his throat.

"Mr. Monroe?"

Rand looked up, eyes wide. "Kiley almost got hit by a car yesterday." His words were a struggle with the implication.

"Would you care to elaborate?"

"Yesterday, or technically, it was the day before, Kiley delivers newspapers on Thursdays. She was delivering when a car almost hit her. She said it crossed the lines like it was headed for her. She sprained her ankle when she fell. Danny, the neighbor boy, had found her and was taking care of her when I got there. He finished her route while I brought her here to be checked."

"Do you have a description of the car?"

Rand thought back to what she said. "A red sports car is all I know. I didn't see it. You'll have to ask Kiley. It's possible that Danny saw it. Listen, I wanted to go home to clean up and get something for Kiley to wear tomorrow when I take her home. With what has happened to her lately, I don't want to leave her alone. Will you be here for a while?"

"I'll be here a little while, but I wouldn't worry. I'll alert security and the nurses' station that only you, myself, and the doctors and nurses are allowed in her room without special authorization. Her room is right across from the nurses' station so they should be able to keep an eye on her.

Rand's uncertainty must have shown. "It's likely I'll still be here when you get back, and no one should be able to find her here so fast. I'll also have a restriction on her information. I want to know who calls."

"All right, I'll be back as soon as I can. By the way, I'd like to get a crew over to Kiley's house to salvage what they can. I don't want Kiley worrying about it. A few of the pieces are heirlooms, but I'm sure everything holds memories. I'm hoping all won't be lost. How soon can they start work?"

Detective Gerome thought a moment. "We should be finished with most of the house by noon. We'll cordon off the other part we don't want them disturbing. Say two to be on the safe side."

Rand nodded, shaking hands with the man. He stopped at the pay phone to call for a taxi before making one last check on Kiley.

Rand walked back in the hospital fifty minutes after he left. He had washed his hair three times and could still smell the smoke. The bag he carried for Kiley wasn't much. He had debated waking his mother to borrow something, but that would have led to questions which would have meant time. So he settled for a pair of gray sweats and thick white socks and a navy jacket. It wouldn't be fashionable but he would buy her anything she wanted later. Deciding not to wait for the elevator, he took the stairs two at a time.

The nurse acknowledged him as he passed her desk. He was pleased to see she was observant even at the early hour, which was late in her shift. It startled him when he pushed the door open to find a man beside her bed. Except for the white coat he was wearing, Rand might have jumped him. His irritation level went up even more when the doctor turned.

"Harvey." His voice was a harsh whisper. "What are you doing here?"

"I was here with a patient when I noticed Ms. Adam's name. I thought that I would check on her." He picked up a chart on the nightstand. "She seems to be resting peacefully. Well, I should be getting back. It seems things have worked out incredibly for you haven't they, Randall? I will see you later."

Rand wondered how he could have hired such an arrogant jerk. Credentials didn't always mean much.

Rand forgot him the moment the door closed. The panel light that hung over Kiley's bed bathed her in a faint glow. Kiley slept peacefully under the low light, turned on her side with her hands tucked under her chin. She looked sweet, innocent and his every dream. The reassuring rhythm of her breathing stirred the blanket.

He wanted to reach down and touch her cheek but was afraid of disturbing her rest. Moving the chair next to the bed, he settled into it. A moment later, he too was asleep.

ꝏꝏ

The woman wouldn't die! What would it take to get rid of her? The first attempt was impulsive. He'd followed her to the bus stop. It had seemed too easy, just a little push. It had been a mistake to use his own car when he tried to run her down. But she wasn't supposed to survive.

He missed the fiery red car with all that power. Well, he would keep it hidden away, and he did like his new car. It was more dignified – it suited him better. But she still had to go!

She was a curse. She should have never survived the fire. He had it all worked out. It was Monroe. He was the trouble. He would have to go too, but he would be more difficult. Handled more carefully, so there wouldn't be any questions. But first, her!

# Chapter Seven

The clattering of trays in the hall woke Kiley. This time it only took her a second before she realized where she was. As she shifted her gaze around the room, it came to rest on Rand. His chair was up against the bed. His shoulder rested against the railing, head tilted her direction, so close, that if she just shifted slightly in the bed, she could press a kiss to his forehead.

Even asleep he didn't look relaxed. There were signs of dark smudges under his eyes, and his chin had a firm set to it. He had obviously showered and changed since she had fallen asleep, but it looked like the only time he had taken on his hair was to run his fingers through it.

For his entire domineering and powerful aura, there was a certain appeal to him that was warming to her. Kiley couldn't call it boyish, for it was too mature, but it was gentleness and something more. Kiley didn't get time to put her finger on it because, as if he could feel her looking at him, he opened his eyes.

A smile crested his lips, as his eyes ran over her. "Hi." His voice was still rugged from the smoke.

"Good morning." Her words came hoarse instead of the softness she was feeling.

Rand immediately reached for her water bottle, helping her with a drink.

The ice water was heavenly on her throat but a little difficult to swallow.

"Thank you." This time her voice was a little better.

"You probably shouldn't try to talk too much."

"Are you implying something?" Her smile took away the bite that might have sounded in her roughened voice.

Rand smiled, lifting his eyebrows wickedly. "Maybe. Good morning." He leaned over brushing his lips against hers.

At that moment, the nurse opened the door. She took Kiley's slightly accelerated vitals then brought in a food tray. Rand excused himself to go outside to make a couple of calls.

No matter that it wasn't even seven a.m., Rand didn't hesitate on making his calls. The first was to his secretary, after informing her he would not be in, he explained about the fire.

"What I want Beth, is for you to arrange a cleaning crew over there to salvage everything they can, and have it cleaned. Then have it taken over to my house and stored in my garage until it can be gone through. I especially want someone with experience with antiques so the repairs can be handled properly. Have them there at two o'clock. That's when the police said they could begin. If you have to pay them time and a half, that's fine. I just want it done as quickly as possible. I don't want Kiley to worry about it."

Rand knew his secretary already had hints of Kiley's importance to him when he had informed her a few days earlier, that if Kiley ever called, he was to be informed immediately, even if he was in a meeting.

His next call was to Wayne, his pilot of the corporate jet, and also a good friend. "Sorry to catch you so early," he apologized. "I need you to be ready to leave in a couple hours."

"I'm supposed to take Vanessa to San Francisco tomorrow shopping," the man said.

Rand grimaced at his step-grandmother's name. The woman was a shrew. "At least it's not New York," he muttered.

"That's next month. She has tickets to see one of the plays before it closes."

"Heavens."

"Yeah," his pilot and friend agreed.

"We'll be back in the morning, so there shouldn't be any trouble. Vanessa wouldn't be seen out until well after noon anyway."

"All right, destination for the flight plans?"

Rand's first thought was for Las Vegas but that wasn't right for Kiley even if it was a quick wedding. "Lake Tahoe, and Wayne, could you arrange for a car there for me?"

"Sure."

"Thanks."

Rand picked up juice and a bagel on his way back to Kiley's room. "Our first breakfast together." He gave her one of his smiles that made her insides flip, as he entered. "What do you think of my romantic setting?"

"Breakfast in bed, service, attention. What more could a girl dream of."

"I thought so."

Except truth be told, the attention was getting a little much. Neither had gotten hardly any sleep, their attempts kept getting interrupted with nurses. They were just settling down for a nap when Gerome came in.

"Don't you ever sleep?" Rand greeted the detective.

"Sometimes I don't think so."

"Kiley, this is Detective Gerome. He's investigating the fire at your house.

"Miss Adams." The detective held out his hand.

"Investigating?" Kiley questioned as she shook his hand.

"I haven't told her yet," Rand said, then took her hand interlocking their fingers. As Gerome talked, her fingers tightened on his hand and the color fled from her face.

"What I need from you at this time is a description of the car that almost hit you two days ago. Mr. Monroe told me about the incident."

"And you think…?"

"It is a little too much of a coincidence."

Kiley proceeded to give everything that she could remember. It was his next question that shocked her. "So Mr. Monroe appeared right after both incidences, do you think that he had –"

"What?" Rand bolted out of his chair.

"No!" Kiley gasped from the bed.

"Mr. Monroe, sit down and try to remember we're in a hospital. If you can't contain yourself, I will ask you to leave."

That was enough to get Rand to drop back into his chair. Fury coursed through his body. The gentle touch of Kiley's hand on his arm helped to bring him back under control.

"Rand, please," she said softly to him. She turned to the detective, her voice became firm. "Rand would never do anything to hurt me. Even if I didn't know it because of the kind of man he is, I would still know it because I have something he would not jeopardize."

"You're certain?"

"Yes."

"Mind if I ask you what?"

Kiley was quiet a moment before answering. "I'm carrying his child."

"Could it be that he doesn't want this child."

"No, sir," she said firmly.

"And may I ask why?"

Again there was a hesitation. "That will be up to Rand to explain, if he wishes. I will just say I am certain he wants it."

When Gerome looked to him, Rand didn't want to answer, but it was important to Kiley's safety. After asking the detective to keep it confidential, he briefly explained. At the end he added, "Kiley's carrying my baby might not have been planned, and you could say I have a fortune riding on this baby, but more importantly, I don't want anything happening to Kiley," he said more for himself because he knew it was true.

The detective nodded. "Actually, I never truly believed Mr. Monroe had anything to do with the attacks, but I had to ask. This opens up a whole new set of possibilities." His brown eyes focused on Rand. "I need a list of names that would stand to gain should Miss Adams die or lose the baby."

"There's a flaw in that," Rand said. "I haven't told anyone about Kiley or the baby yet."

"There is another flaw." Kiley drew the men's attention back to her. "The first attack happened even before I met Rand, and I didn't know about the baby." She then described being pushed in front of the bus.

Gerome nodded. "I'll look into it, just in case the first was not truly an accident. I'll be in touch."

"Thank you."

Rand handed him a list of names, then he walked him out. "This is my card with my cell phone and home number written on back, if you need to reach us. For the next twenty-four hours we will be out of town, but please keep me informed."

Gerome agreed. "No hard feelings over the questions in there?"

"No, you were doing your job. The important thing here is keeping Kiley safe."

"You were right about what you said earlier, about meeting her. I can't see her having an enemy. You're a very lucky man."

"I know." Rand watched the man walk away.

Rand waited outside while a nurse helped Kiley into a bath. They hardly got settled back down when the doctor came in and sent Rand back out. Rand used the time to run down to the pharmacy across the street for more prenatal vitamins and another pair of crutches for her. By the time he got back, she was cleared to leave the hospital with a caution to rest as much as possible for a couple days, and take it easy on talking for a day or two, which was all right with Rand. He could only think of two words he wanted her to say—"I do".

With all the check out papers to sign and confusion at the hospital, it was almost eleven before the nurse wheeled her out while Rand pulled his car up to the front.

Kiley looked adorable in his sweats, Rand thought as he pulled his car up to the curb. They totally obliterated her shape. The shoulders hung down on the sides almost to her elbows, the sleeves had to be rolled up about six inches. Kiley had to cinch the waist as much as possible, and they still hung on her.

She really hadn't appreciated it when he told her she could grow to fit them, but he'd caught the secret smile that crossed her lips just before he turned his back. He knew she'd been thinking of his baby growing in her. The thought that she found pleasure in it warmed him.

So had the sweet look she'd given him when he'd knelt next to the bed, where her legs hung over, to roll up the pant legs and slid on the socks he brought. He couldn't help think as low as the top hung, he should have brought one of his shirts and she could have worn it as a dress. She looked so small and vulnerable.

"This isn't the way to my house," were the first words out of her mouth once they left the hospital.

"I wasn't headed there," he answered simply.

"Rand, I need to go home." Kiley could tell he was reluctant. "Please, Rand, I really need to. There is a lot that I need to do."

"Yes – rest, like the doctor said."

"I will rest when I've cleaned up my house."

"You don't have to worry about that. I already have a crew coming in to do that. They will be there as soon as the police will allow."

"But …," the look he gave her stopped her argument. "It's bad isn't it? All the damage." She looked up at him.

"Don't worry about it. They'll salvage what they can."

"I still need to go."

Rand was finding he really had a problem denying her. "Kiley."

"Please. I at least need my purse."

He turned at the next corner having to agree with that, though he wasn't happy until he felt Kiley's hand slid over his on the gearshift. He glanced toward her.

"Thank you." She squeezed down lightly.

So what if he was having a problem denying her, maybe it wasn't so bad.

Fifteen minutes later, when he saw the look on Kiley's face as they pulled up in front of her house, he wished he would have stayed firm. He tried to tell himself that she had to face it sometime, but he just wished she had waited until he had it cleaned up.

"Kiley, we can go now," he said when she just sat there, eyes fixed on her burned house. Without any comment, Kiley reached for the door handle. Rand came out and around the car in a flash, afraid in her stupor she would forget her ankle and step down on it. He was right, just making it in time to catch her when she started to step out. He balanced her with his body while he reached for her crutches.

The light of day told the true story. Nearly a quarter of the house was totally destroyed, another half showed signs of the fire and water damage. It was a miracle Rand had gotten them both out alive.

With a tremor of fear, Kiley turned into him. No sobs came. She just clung to him, as she stared at what had been her home. She didn't have a home now, and she might have lost her life.

That he might have lost her was what frightened Rand and had him clinging to her. After a time, he turned his head pressing kisses against the side of her head. "It's all right baby."

"You could have died." She shivered, burrowing deeper against him.

"I didn't, and you didn't, and that's what is important."

She nodded, and turned to press her lips to his. Rand was shocked by the first kiss she'd instigated, then was more surprised by the reaction he felt. His body tingled as if she had merged in every part of him with her loving essence. He knew he could never purge her from his body. Nor did he want to, he thought greedily as he took what she offered and attempted to give back of himself.

Kiley felt singed when she pulled back, but the heat felt wonderful. The longing consumed all the way to her heart. She hoped it wouldn't destroy her, but she knew it might, and she would be as powerless to stop it as her house had been against the flames of the fire.

"Kiley!" The sound of her name being called drew her away from Rand's body. "Kiley!" She turned to the boy running down the street. "You're all right. It was so scary, the firemen and everything. Mom called the hospital for me, but they would only say you were stable and resting. You should have seen it. The police have been here, too."

"Hi, Danny," she gave the boy a hug.

He beamed at her then at Rand. "Mr. Gordon said that you saved Kiley. That there was fire all around you and that you handed Kiley out to the firemen then collapsed out after her." There was a strong tone of hero worship in the boy's voice. "Did you burn your arm?" He motioned to the bandage.

"No, cut it on glass from the window. Had to have a few stitches."

"I fell on a broken bottle and had to have stitches in my knee once. It killed. They aren't letting anyone near the house yet."

"It's not safe, and they're investigating for evidence," Kiley said matter-of-factly, looking up at her home.

"Yeah, I talked to one of the policemen. He asked about the car, too. Do they really think someone is trying to hurt you?"

Rand squeezed her against him and answered for her. "They don't know yet."

"What are you going to do?"

"We're moving up the wedding so I can keep Kiley with me." He was pleased that Kiley didn't protest.

"You'll take care of her," Danny stated with certain knowledge.

"I will," Rand added his promise.

Tightening his hold on her, he slid his hand over her abdomen and the child developing there. He would take care of her and be the best husband and father he could.

Together they crossed the street. Yellow police tape flapped in the light breeze. Kiley kept her eyes from the blackened end of the house, but the smell of the smoke lingered heavily in the air. The front door showed damage of being forced open. They stood in the entry and looked around. The carpet was wet and filthy.

"Did you not see the police tape?"

The stern voice had Kiley turning with a jerk that almost unbalanced her.

"This is Miss Adams," Rand spoke up before Kiley could find her voice.

A man with a badge hooked to his belt stepped from the hallway. "Sorry, ma'am. We're just about finished here."

"We'd like to get a couple things," Rand again asked for her.

"There's not much worth salvaging down there."

Rand nodded. "We just need her purse and ID. It should be in the closet."

"Sure, I just have to check the ID and have you sign for it."

"A cleaning crew will be here in an hour or so to move the antiques and personal items that can be salvaged out," Rand informed the officer.

"No problem. We'll tape off where we don't want them to cross. The investigation is pretty much finished here."

"Thanks." He turned back to Kiley. She stood frozen, staring down the blackened hall. "Kiley."

"I was upset when you had to cut the leg of my old jeans, now…" Tears built up in her eyes but didn't fall.

Rand cursed under his breath. Opening the closet door, he took out Kiley's purse, opened the wallet and showed her ID to the officer.

As soon as Kiley signed the release form, Rand slid his arm back around her. "Come on, let's go."

She didn't say a word as he directed her out, staying close in case she slipped. She hardly acknowledged Danny's good-bye. Rand tried to give the boy a reassuring look, knowing that he had picked up the difference in her mood.

Rand really began to worry when Kiley remain quiet all the way to the airport and made no comment when he scooped her into his arms and carried her onto the jet. She didn't seem to notice the craft's plush leather seats or Wayne standing in the doorway to the cock-pit.

Rand nodded to the man and lowered Kiley into a seat. He did up the buckle then reach for a blanket to tuck around her. With a gentle hand he brushed her hair back from her cheek, bent over and kissed it. "Go to sleep, sweetheart," he whispered then leaned forward and brushed a kiss across her forehead this time.

At Wayne's looked, he stepped to the pilot.

"Is there something wrong?" his pilot and friend asked as he eyed Kiley.

It was obvious the man was trying to make sense of the near comatose woman. "Yes. Someone tried to burn down Kiley's house last night with her in it." The words sent a chill down his back. "She was handling things fine until we stopped and looked at her house. That on top of other things has hit her hard. That's one of the reasons I want to get her away."

"I don't blame you."

"I need to grab her crutches then we can go."

The man nodded and went in the cockpit.

Kiley was asleep by the time they were in the air. Rand used the time to pull out his computer to make arrangements for the wedding.

When they landed, Rand left Kiley long enough to pick up the rental car. Kiley aroused enough to make it to the car, then slipped back into the daze she'd been in the last three hours. Rand wasn't even sure she noticed the incredible emerald lake they were driving around or the pine-covered hillside. It troubled him because it wasn't like Kiley not to notice beauty.

Finally, unable to ignore the concern any longer, he pulled off on a scenic outlook. Walking around the car, he opened the door and scooped her out, not bothering with her crutches. He carried her over to a large boulder beneath a tall ponderosa pine.

"Look at it Kiley." He pointed out at the lake. When she failed to look, he cupped her face firmly in his hands.

"Look at it." He forced her head up but knew she wasn't seeing. "Look at me. Please, Kiley, look at me," he pleaded.

Slowly her eyes came up to his face. Frustrated, he pressed his mouth to hers. It was not a gentle kiss or even a passionate one. It was rough and firm, born out of desperation. No response seemed to come from her. Rand deepened the kiss.

Over a minute, still nothing happened. He was about to give up when he felt her begin to come alive and return the pressure. As he eased, she came in for more. Her mouth opened under his coaxing, and he slipped in. A groan escaped from her throat, and Rand heard one of his own slip free in answer.

She was unbelievably sweet and innocent. He broke away from her lips to run kisses along her cheek and down her neck. He heard her gasp his name, and his heart soared. Coming back up, he showered her face with kisses.

"My Kiley, sweetheart," he pressed his lips to hers once more, then tucked her against his chest, running his hands up and down her back.

For several minutes, they sat like that. In the distance, cars raced by but didn't intrude on their private world.

"Rand, where are we?" Her whispered voice was a balm to his soul.

"Lake Tahoe." He pressed a kiss to her cheek.

"Lake Tahoe?" she questioned back, lifting her head to look up to him with eyes as blue as the sky.

"We're getting married here in a couple hours," he told her gently.

"Married?"

"Yes, my little parrot, and if we don't get busy and go shopping, you'll end up getting married in my baggie sweats."

"Married?" Kiley repeated again, still stunned.

"Married," he said firmly, picking her up to head back to the car.

"Oh, Rand, look at the lake," she said over his shoulder. He turned with her cradled in his arms.

"It is beautiful isn't it," he agreed, relieved that she was returning to her normal self.

"Gorgeous, I've never been here before. Actually, I've never been much of anywhere, except the trip to meet my grandparents once."

"You just name where you want to go, and I'll take you." His voice grew husky.

"Here's nice." She sighed, laying her head on his shoulder.

Rand couldn't agree more. Right here was very nice with Kiley in his arms. "Let's go find you something to wear." He headed back to the car.

As he settled her into the seat, she looked up. "Rand, I'm so tired."

He reached out and touched her cheek. "Would you like to go to the hotel and take a nap?"

"Yes, please."

"All right, we should be at the hotel in about ten minutes."

This time as he drove, her head was laid back against the seat, but she went on and on about how beautiful the view was. At the hotel it only took a matter of minutes to have them registered into the suite. Neither paid any attention to the looks Kiley was receiving in the elegant lobby on crutches, wearing Rand's oversized sweats.

"Would you like something from room service?" he asked as they entered the suite.

"No, just sleep. Oh!" Kiley looked wide-eyed at the room that greeted her.

"Do you like it?"

"It's lovely. I've only seen rooms like this on TV." Thick, cream carpet covered the floor. Rose, hunter-green and cream colors accented the traditional cherry-wood furniture. A small table in the middle of the room had a large bouquet of fresh flowers. Immediately, Kiley headed to them to smell, bringing a smile to Rand's face. Of all the glamour and expense, it was simple flowers that drew Kiley most.

He went to open the doors to the master bedroom. "You really should have something to eat. You haven't had anything since breakfast."

"I just want to sleep."

"This way then," he said, holding the doors open. The same rich colors continued in the bedroom, but the main focal point on the other side of the king-size bed was the view of the lake outside the glass doors.

"Wow." She crossed the room fumbling awkwardly between the crutches and the lock until Rand laid his hand over hers, taking over opening the door. The fresh smell of pine and the sound of birds greeted them.

Kiley looked over the lake. "How beautiful." She leaned over, placing a kiss on his cheek. "Thank you." She sounded as if she was giving him credit for the whole lake.

"You're welcome." He smiled. "Now, come lay down." He steered her back inside. "I'll be back in a while, you just rest." He pulled back the quilt and helped her ease down. Tucking her in, he pressed a kiss to her forehead. "Sleep well."

Kiley lay looking out the window only a few minutes before her eyes drifted close. Her last thought was that maybe this all was a dream.

CஜலD

The shop, the woman at the front desk directed him to, was perfect. Rand saw the dress he wanted the moment he walked through the door. It wasn't a true wedding dress, but it would be right for Kiley. White, simple, short-sleeved but the bottom flared out with two lengths of material that would swirl just above her ankle.

The size was the most difficult thing, so he did what any man would do in the situation. He pointed out another woman that was about Kiley's size. Then he held out his hands, picturing them as if they were going around Kiley's waist, to decide if it was right.

Shoes were a more difficult problem, so at the suggestion of the salesperson, he picked a low heel adjustable sandal in two different sizes. As he shopped for lingerie, Rand picked up quite a few stares, but he was so fixed on picking what was right for Kiley he didn't care. Several times as he picked up articles he almost groaned aloud at the thought of seeing her in just the scraps of satin and lace. He knew he would have fantasies of her in the thigh-length satin nightgown and wondered how long it would be until he could make his marriage real and Kiley his. Running his fingers over the soft satin of the virginal white nightgown, the thought came – *only his.*

The next thing on his list was a ring. The choice again was easy the moment he saw it. The large diamond was sided by blue sapphires the color of Kiley's eyes. When the wedding band was added, the diamond would be circled in the blue like he felt when he looked in to Kiley's eyes.

Heavens, he was turning into a romantic. Wouldn't his mother, who had been after him forever about being too serious and all business, be surprised? Rand also couldn't resist the necklace, a drop shape diamond sided with sapphires, and earrings to match.

Now she would need personal basic items. Luckily Kiley didn't wear much makeup and he had seen lipstick in her purse, so he wouldn't worry about makeup. He picked up a toothbrush, toothpaste, brush and a curling iron at the clerk's suggestion then headed to the men's department for him. Twenty minutes later, he came out wearing a loose-fitting white shirt and new slacks, giving him a kind of pirate look he decided he liked.

The last stop on the way back to the hotel was to pick up flowers, which Rand discovered he should have done first. But he was assured that they would be done in half an hour so he decided to take the time to go check out the wedding chapel he'd found on line. It too, he decided, was perfect except for one change. Kiley would prefer the setting of the gazebo out back that was covered with flowers. He could see her there, among the blossoms.

He made a mental note to contact a contractor to build a gazebo behind his house. His yard could use some landscaping. Maybe that would give Kiley something to do that would make her happy.

Within a little under three hours, Rand walked back into their suite. Kiley was still asleep where he'd left her. He couldn't help take a minute to watch her before settling next to her on the bed.

"Kiley." He ran his finger along her cheek. "Kiley sweetheart, wake up." With a deep breath, she stretched, yawned, and then opened her eyes. Rand's heart caught at the smile that crossed her face when she saw him. Yes, Kiley would be his. "Hi. Sorry, but it's time to change."

"Change?" The rasping caused by the smoke was gone from her voice, leaving it only soft and smooth as ever.

"The wedding."

"Today?" With his nod, she added, "Now?"

"Yes."

"But I can't Rand, look at me."

"I think you look beautiful." And she did to him.

"I can't get married like this, please."

Rand could see the tears rising in her eyes and decided it was not the time to tease her. "Then you'll have to change. Stay here."

She was sitting up in the bed when he retrieved the bags from the other room. First, he handed her the bag filled with the brush, comb, and other personal items he'd purchased, along with raspberry bubble bath and lotion that he had added. Kiley blushed when she opened the bag of lingerie, but Rand notice her run her finger discreetly over the silky nightgown.

When he removed the dress from the garment bag, Kiley's reaction was everything he hoped. Her mouth made a perfect O, and her eyes sparkled as he laid it across the foot of the bed. Tears glistened in her eyes as she looked up at him, but this time, by her countenance, he knew they were happy tears.

"Thank you."

"You're welcome." It was all he could do not to take her in his arms. Rand knew if he did he'd be hard pressed to release her again. He did lean forward and brush his lips over hers. "Can you make it into the bath okay?"

Her head moved up and down slowly, her eyes not leaving his face. He wanted to kiss her again, but knew if he started now, he wouldn't stop.

# Chapter Eight

As Kiley settled in the hot perfumed water, she thought of the items on her bed. She could still feel the silky gown in her fingers and couldn't help think about Rand buying it for her, along with all the other things in the bag. She felt herself blush again, especially at the thoughts of the camisole and underwear.

All were unlike the plain, utilitarian undergarments she normally wore. So many times she'd been tempted to buy something so daring, but never could quite bring herself to. Money had always been an issue. Though, once she had promised herself when she could, she would get herself a beautiful nightgown, and the one on the bed could have been the one from her dreams.

Why Rand had chosen that particular nightgown, she didn't know, but she wondered if he wanted to see her in it.

 CB&O

Rand tried to wait patiently for Kiley. After he had showered and changed, he tried to lie down on the couch and take a nap, but it was no good. Coming to his feet, he paced the cream carpet.

It had only been forty-five minutes since he had left her. He wasn't sure how long she would take. His mother allotted at least two hours to prep for a special occasion, but Kiley wasn't his mother. She wasn't like any woman he knew.

Rand made two more trips across the floor when he heard the door open. Kiley stood in the doorway. The smile she gave him was hesitant, as if waiting for his approval, but there was no way in the world Rand could give it. Nothing could get past the lump in his throat.

Her golden hair hung loose and free down her back. He knew the dress would look good on her, but not even his imagination had prepared him for the sight of her. The top clung to her figure as the bottom blossomed out to flow down around her ankles. White was definitely a color for her. She looked like an angel. Though his reaction to her was undoubtedly earthy − most preachers would say downright carnal or sinful− but to Rand, it was heavenly.

That was the word that made it out. "Heavenly." At her surprise, he continued. "You look like an angel. I'm almost afraid to blink in case you disappear."

Kiley caught her lip between her teeth, making him almost groan aloud. "I'm sorry I kept you waiting."

Rand laughed. "You didn't, but any wait would have been worth it. You're beautiful."

"Thank you. You look pretty good yourself."

"You don't mind my not wearing a suit or a tux? I'm in them all the time, and today's just for you and me."

If Kiley needed another sign she loved him and marrying him was right, she'd just received it in the 'today is just for you and me'. At a big fancy wedding, she would have been uncomfortable. Her grandmother was the only person she would have missed being here with her. She froze. "Rand, won't your family miss being here?"

"My mother will accept it, and she is the only one that matters. I have something for you. Come here."

Kiley retrieved her crutches leaning on the inside of the door and made her way to him.

"I think this should be done on bent knee."

Stunned, Kiley watched Rand lower himself before her.

"Kiley, I don't want to lose you. Will you marry me?" He slid the ring on her trembling finger. Her bottom lip again caught in her teeth for only a brief moment as he rose, coming up to kiss her. When he pulled back from the kiss, he smiled down. "Does this mean yes?"

"Yes." Kiley kissed him this time in answer.

"Enough of that, or you won't make it to the ceremony without being ravished first. I have a wedding present for you too." He reached for the long box on the table, handing it to her.

Kiley's hands trembled as she opened it. "Rand," she gasped at the earrings and necklace that matched the sparkling ring on her finger. Though the necklace hung like a drop on a simple white gold chain, it was incredibly beautiful and she guessed expensive. "I ... I can't ..."

"It's your wedding present. As soon as I saw it, I wanted it for you. It matches the ring on your finger and your eyes."

Before Kiley could say more, he lifted the necklace from its velvet lined box. His fingers caressed her neck as he fastened the clasp. Her trembling increased as his fingers traced their way slowly back around to where the pendant hung. Her breath caught and eyes closed as his fingers touched the stone just over the valley between her breasts.

Next he picked up an earring, placing it in her ear. He followed it with a gentle kiss. Kiley's hands came to his shoulders for balance. A small groan escaped her as he slipped the second earring in.

Rand knew without a doubt Kiley was his for the taking, except that he wanted her legally, lawfully his. His lips came back to hers one more time before he broke away.

She looked up at him, her big blue eyes touched with sadness.

"Kiley?"

"I don't have anything for you."

"Oh, sweetheart you are everything I want, everything I never thought that I would have."

"But –"

"Shh," he placed a finger over the lips still moist from his kiss. "We'll stop and get me a ring later. All right."

He waited until she nodded.

"Good! I think we are about ready to go, except for these," he said, lifting the bouquet from the table.

"Oh, Rand." Tears filled her eyes at the flowers – a cluster of different lilies and other bright blooms tied together with a ribbon.

"Diamonds and sapphires take her breath away, but flowers bring her to tears," he joked.

"No. You take my breath away." Realizing what she said, she looked down in embarrassment.

With his hand under her chin, he tilted it up. "That's good to know." He brushed her lips with another kiss. "Shall we go?"

Kiley knew he was giving her one last out, but she wasn't taking it. She couldn't. For better or worse, she loved him and she was going to try to make Rand as happy as she was with him.

CR&

Kiley fell in love with the little chapel the instant she saw it. But when Rand led her around back to the gazebo covered with flowers, she knew that was where she wanted to be married. She was trying to figure out how to ask if they could be married there instead of inside, when Rand suggested it.

A few minute later, they stood together in the little white structure, surrounded by the flowers of the quaint gardens. Birds provided the music as they exchanged their vows. They might have only known each other a week, but the vows were made from their hearts.

After Rand slid the ring on her finger and they were pronounced husband and wife, he gave her a kiss that he hoped would seal her to him and leave no doubt of his feelings and desires. Though he still felt a little nervous about hurrying Kiley into marriage when there were so many upheavals in her life, he couldn't regret it, especially when she gave herself over to him so totally in the kiss. He swung her up in his arms, cradling her to him taking the kiss to another level until he remembered where they were.

Carefully he set her down so they could sign the papers that made her legally his. Her fingers trembled slightly as she signed her name, but the smile she gave him as she raised her head was brilliant. Unable to resist, Rand reached for her again, lifting her into his arms.

He carried her through the garden while the minister's wife, who had been one of the witnesses, continued to take pictures as she had done throughout the ceremony. He kissed Kiley under a shade tree then stopped so she could smell the flowers. He pressed his face into her neck to breathe in the fragrance of her, which was sweeter to him than any flower.

They stayed in the garden, taking private, special time until they couldn't delay leaving any longer. He carried her to the car, leaving her only long enough to retrieve her crutches and the disk of photos, thanking the woman for her thoughtfulness.

Rand's desire was to head back to the hotel, but he promised himself that he wouldn't rush Kiley anymore. He didn't want her waking up in a couple days or weeks uncertain, doubting herself, and regretting marrying him. So instead, he headed to the jeweler where he'd purchased her ring.

The man greeted them warmly as they entered. "Lovely, perfect," he commented on the necklace that glistened around her throat. "Is there a problem with the ring?"

"No, it's perfect." Rand smiled, noticing Kiley cover it protectively. "What we're looking for now is a wedding band for me."

They followed him to the counter. Rand helped Kiley settle in a chair, and then he leaned over her.

"What do you prefer?" She looked up to him.

"You pick a couple out first and I'll narrow it down." He suggested, wanting the choice to be hers.

She hesitated, and then nodded. Turning back, she studied the rings. She skipped over the bands, as none of them seemed right. Quite a few with diamonds seem a bit ostentatious, which was not Rand. He was strong, forceful but not showy. Her eyes rested on a ring with a small diamond sided by two deep-blue sapphires. The stones were nestled in white gold with yellow gold around the band. She continued to look but her eyes kept coming back to it. It was rich but not showy. So like him, an original unlike any others.

"That one, please."

The man placed it on the counter, and without a word, Rand picked it up and removed it from the box, placed it in Kiley's hand for her to slide on him. With unsteady fingers, she slid it over his finger where it rested perfectly. Kiley's breath caught as Rand intertwined their fingers. Lifting his other hand to her chin, he tilted it up as he lowered his head to take possession of her mouth, resealing the promise of their vows.

There was no question about it. The ring was there to stay.

CRBD

At the restaurant, Rand requested a table by the window where they could watch the setting sun over the lake. Hues of red, gold and orange filled the sky. It seemed impossible that a day, which had started out in the hospital as one of the worst days in her life, could end as the most wonderful day in her entire life.

Kiley couldn't believe so much could happen in one day. She looked over to Rand to find him watching her. Unable to pull her eyes away, warmth rushed through her body quickening her heart.

"Thank you, Rand." It didn't seem enough to say for what she felt. "Thank you for everything."

His hand covered hers on the table, lacing their fingers together. They gazed at each other then, in silent communication, both turned and watched the last sliver of the sun drop behind the mountains.

"Ready to go?" His voice was low and husky.

Kiley nodded, and he helped her stand. "I will be happy to be rid of these crutches," she forced a little laugh as she maneuvered around a table barely missing a chair leg.

"Just a few more days." She felt his hand brush her back. Her heart pounded.

She tried to think of something else to say, wondering if he could tell how nervous she was thinking about what would happen back at the hotel. Surprisingly though, as the car started her eyelids began to droop. By the time they reached the hotel, she was asleep.

Rand roused her getting her out of the car, but it was still hard for her to keep her eyes open. In the elevator, she snuggled against him, letting her eyes close again only to force them open again when she heard the chime announcing the arrival at their floor. It was her wedding night, but even her nervousness was tempered with weariness.

Rand startled her when he snagged a hold of her crutches and swung her up into his arms. "Tradition," was all he said as he carried her to their suite. Inside, he easy her back down in the middle of the room. Repositioning her crutches, he kept an arm around her as he directed her to the master bedroom.

Rand wasn't quite sure how to broach the subject of wanting to consummate their marriage. The kisses he had given her had been returned with fervor. She had said she loved him. He felt she desired him, but as much he wanted to make love to her, he'd promised to be patient.

If he didn't love her and care for her so much it might have been easy to take advantage of her, but he did love her. He cared for her sweet innocence, and every movement she made, said that she was weak and vulnerable, and at that moment half asleep. He couldn't take advantage of her in that state.

"Kiley."

She raised her head when he said her name.

"Will you need any help getting ready for bed?" His voice sounded strained.

"I can manage." She blushed slightly.

"All right," he eased her on the bed. "I'll be back it a minute." Not sure how he found the willpower, he made it to the door, closing it firmly behind him before he gave into his desire.

ఇళ

Kiley looked at the door, wondering if he meant that he would be back to sleep with her. A flash of excitement burst through her tired body. After all, they were married. She was his wife. That wasn't the only reason she wanted to be with him. She loved him and wanted to be his in every sense of the word.

She tried not to wonder if he wanted her the same way. It was pretty unlikely. Rand Monroe could have any woman he wanted. Why would he want her with dishwater-blonde hair of no special style, average height, average weight, average look, and average intelligence? She was really beginning to hate the word average, but she knew that was best what described her. She didn't even know how to wear make-up like most women.

Pushing her insecurities away, she carefully removed the necklace and earrings. She put them on the dresser then stopped to finger her ring. That would stay where it was.

Catching a glimpse of herself in the mirror, she twisted back and forth watching the dress. Even the crutches didn't hamper the way it floated around her ankles. She loved how the dress looked, and more importantly, Rand seemed to like it on her. He seemed to like her. His kisses still burned on her lips.

She didn't have the experience to know if they meant the same to him as they did to her. Her smile tilted with self-directed mirth. She really was naïve.

Sliding out of the dress, she hung it up, stopping to look at herself again in the mirror. She ran her fingers over the satin camisole, feeling a little more confidence at what she saw there.

Her shape was pretty good, not 'built' or curvy but lean, trim, maybe too much so, but that wouldn't last long. In a few months, her body would start to swell with the baby, Rand's baby. Was she trying to forget what was important to him? Her self-doubt said, *You're just packaging.*

*No!* She fought back with her heart. Rand cared for her. He wouldn't have kissed her, talked to her like he did if he didn't care. Rand could never be that dishonest. He cared for her, and she loved him. She had to have faith in that.

With conviction, she changed into the white nightgown, brushed her hair and teeth and settled on the bed to wait for Rand. The conviction didn't hold long once she lay down. Weariness crept back through her body. The naps did nothing to stay the after-effects of the night before. Hardly ten minutes passed before her eyelids closed, and Kiley drifted to sleep with her thoughts on Rand.

ⵣ

Rand was not sure how he found the will power to force himself from the room. He paced the floor, his attention on the door and the fact that Kiley was on the other side of it. He shoved his fingers through his hair and tipped his head back, letting out a long breath.

Rand hoped he had given her enough time because he couldn't wait any longer. He knocked softly on the door. When there was no answer, he knocked again a little harder. "Kiley?" He waited. "Kiley?" he repeated the call. With a twinge of uncertainty, he turned the handle and pushed open the door.

The vision that greeted him stole his breath away, though it was concern that had him crossing to the bed. Kiley lay stretched out over the quilt, her silky hair fanned out around her head. Long, shapely legs were exposed from thigh down. The white gown promised more than it hid. Gentle breaths pressed her breasts temptingly against the thin material that covered them. They called for his touch, his caress.

Drawing on what honor and will power he had left, Rand slid one arm under her enough to raise her. Kiley cuddled into his chest mumbling something that could have been his name. A groan rumbled deep in his throat.

Setting his jaw, he pulled down the duvet and settled her in the bed, then brought the cover up to hide her from his view. Though, it was far too late to make a difference, the sight of her was etched in his mind where it would be forever.

"It's going to be another long night." Rand said to himself as he bent down and brushed a kiss across her cheek. "Sleep well, my darling," he whispered

"Rand." This time his name was audible though she was deep asleep.

"Sorry, sweetheart, the only honeymoon tonight will be in our dreams." He gave her another kiss and headed for another cold shower.

 C380

"Kiley, sweetheart."

Kiley stirred and turned her head toward the gentle stroke against her cheek. She stretched, too content to open her eyes. She could feel the sunlight from the window warming her bed.

In her dreams, Rand was beside her. He kissed her, touched her so that her heart raced. She didn't want to let go of the dream. She wanted Rand to want her.

"Sorry, sweetheart, but it's time to wake up. We have a plane to catch." Rand ran his finger over her cheek then groaned as Kiley stretched again. It sounded like a purr under his caress, like a contented cat.

He should have awakened her from the doorway. Never should he have entered the bedroom or looked down at her in the golden glow of the morning light. The vision of her the night before was enough to keep him awake and tense for hours, but with the light turning her hair into a halo of gold, he stifled another groan.

Her dark lashes fluttered and opened, a smile crested her lips when she saw him. It nearly ripped him apart. "Darling, you look at me like that, and I'll not be responsible for the consequences."

"What consequences?" she asked in a dreamy softness.

"Ah, love you are going to get yourself into trouble asking questions like that. We have a plane to catch, or I'm going to have to face my wicked step-grandmother."

"I'd rather stay in bed," she sighed. "I was dreaming."

Rand knew it was dangerous, but he couldn't stop himself. "What were you dreaming?"

"You were holding me, touching me."

This time he did groan out loud. She was killing him. "Kiley." He put a finger over her lips before she could say another word. "I've already had two cold showers since last night, and now I'm going to be on my way to a third. I only have so much willpower, and I have about reached the end of it."

He groaned again when she rubbed her cheek against his palm. "Sweetheart, I promised myself to be patient and not hurry you, but you are tearing me apart. I want to make love to you like I have never wanted anything else, but I will not risk losing you. Now we have to get going so we can get you some clothes before we go to the airport."

Kiley couldn't believe what he'd said. He wanted her. That he was trying to be noble. Unable to stop herself, she pressed her lips against the finger that rested against them. "Why would you lose me?" she asked when he jerked his hand away.

"You need time."

"I love you." Her words went right to his soul.

Rand froze, not quite sure if she was saying what he thought she was. "Kiley?"

"I want to be yours."

"Are you certain?"

"Yes."

"You have to be certain, because once we make love, our marriage stands. The choice is yours Kiley. I want you to be certain."

She smiled up at him confidently. "I'm sure. I think I fell in love with you that first day. I mean in the waiting room, when I hit you with the door, but I have known for certain for days now. There will never be anyone else for me."

"You hit me with more than the door that day. I couldn't get you out of my mind, but Kiley, I promise you I will wait if you want. I love you."

"I don't want to wait, Rand. I want to be yours."

"Oh sweetheart, I want that too." He kissed her gently, sliding his body down beside her. "I love you." He kissed her again, sliding his arms around her, feeling the tremors running though her body. "It will be all right, I promise."

Kiley bit her bottom lip that he'd just kissed and nodded.

"You're nervous," he said running his finger over her hair.

"Yes."

"There is nothing to be nervous about. It's just me."

"But what if I don't …," she looked away embarrassed.

"Don't what?" He laid a finger on her chin, turning it back to him.

"I don't know what to do to … to please you."

"Oh, sweetheart," he folded her into his arms. "Everything you do pleases me, but don't worry. I think we'll be just fine." His lips gently caressed hers. "Just relax and let me love you," he said between kisses.

# Chapter Nine

Kiley lay content in Rand's arms, her head rested on his chest while she ran her hand across it. Now that she had touched him, she couldn't seem to get enough. Rand didn't seem to mind, in return his hands moved lightly over her. She felt his lips brush her temple.

"Are you all right?" He kissed the side of her head.

"I'm wonderful."

"I'm glad, because I don't think we're going to have time to do any shopping."

"We can shop at home." Kiley pressed her lips against his bare chest, enjoying the tickling of the hair that dusted his chest. She added more kisses, and her hands joined in running over the hard muscle.

"Kiley." Rand caught her fingers and brought them to his mouth. He kissed and suckled each digit, producing a small gasp then a moan from her. Her body quivered again, her lips found his heated skin. "If you don't stop that, you're not even going to get breakfast, and I will run the risk of Vanessa's wrath."

"That's the second time you mentioned her wrath. Is she that bad?" Kiley asked while continuing to administer kisses.

"Later," Rand growled, shifting abruptly so she was under him. "Let's think of something more pleasant."

◠◡

It ended that they had to dress and head straight to the airport. Kiley wore the dress she was married in.

Wayne was waiting with the plane ready to go when they rushed up.

"Sorry," Kiley blushed as she moved passed him.

"Good morning. You look like you're feeling better today."

"Yes, I feel great today." She looked back at Rand, catching the grin he gave her.

Unfortunately, it didn't last long. The late breakfast, which consisted of a donut and juice they ate once the plane got into the air, set off a touch of morning sickness, so she spent the entire flight slightly nauseous.

Looking out the window helped a little, but she spent most of the time lying back against the seat and Rand's shoulder while he read over some corporate papers. Kiley never once felt left out as, every few minutes, Rand's lips would find their way to her temple, cheek or dip down to her lips. His hands never seemed to still on her arm. Just before landing, he put his work away.

"You play havoc with my concentration." He caught her hand bringing it to his lips.

"I didn't do anything."

"You didn't have to."

"Sorry, I can move over there." She was aware of the teasing in her voice. Turning her hand, she caressed his face. There was a slight roughness to it that was so intriguing but nothing to compare with the feelings the coursed within her. Her heart burst at the thought of how much she loved him. She didn't doubt now he loved her. It had been in each touch and caress as he taught her about physical love

"I don't think so. I want you right where you are." He kissed her deeply. "Are you hungry?" he asked when he finally broke the kiss.

"Ravenous."

"Me to, but we'll get something to eat and do some shopping for you before we go home, or we'll never get back out again today."

Kiley couldn't keep back the blush that colored her cheeks at his double entendre, but suspected Rand was right as he drew her back into his arms. Neither realized they'd landed until Wayne walked back into the cabin, clearing his throat.

"Thanks, Wayne." Rand shook hands with the pilot while Kiley composed herself.

"Any time, congratulations."

"Thank you."

"Nice meeting you Kiley."

"Nice to meet you too." She accepted his hand.

"Do I get to kiss the bride?"

She laughed, leaning forward to receive a kiss on the cheek.

"I'd say you really lucked out man." Wayne turned back to Rand.

"I'd have to agree with you. Listen, I've got a favor to ask. Can you keep everything about our getting married to yourself for a couple days?"

"Mum's the word." Wayne held up his fingers making a pledge.

"I hope I didn't get you in trouble with Vanessa." He hated to think what his step-grandmother would be like if she had to wait for the plane to be readied.

Wayne shrugged. "She won't be here for at least an hour. That gives me plenty time to do the paper work and even grab some lunch. Either way, it makes no different to me. I just go into the cockpit and put on the headphones. It's whoever she drags with her who will have to listen to her complaints."

Rand laughed. "Thanks." He waved as he helped Kiley off the plane.

"Hey, you don't happen to have a sister do you?" the pilot called out behind them.

"No," Kiley answered with a smile.

"Sorry, she's one of a kind," Rand grinned back over his shoulder.

"Some guys get all the luck." Wayne's words followed them to the car.

"Is your stepmother really like that?" Kiley asked once settled in her seat.

"Step-grandmother, and she's precisely like that. Just wait until you meet her. She divides her time between the spa, shopping, and going out to her society functions, which is more to be seen there than to help. I don't know how my grandfather ever ended up with her. He was usually so level-headed and conservative."

"Is this the man who required an heir within a year out of you?"

Rand winced and Kiley grabbed his hand. "I'm sorry." Rand loved his grandfather like she loved her grandmother.

Rand shook his head and brought her hand to his lips. "It's true, but in all fairness, I don't think he was intending to die when he did. I think he added that to his new will to put a little pressure on me. He knew I was over-working and putting my personal life aside. He wanted me happy, and I can't say I regret what he did because even if it was an accident, it still gave me you. He was right. I'm seeing things a little differently now."

He kissed her fingers again before shifting to press her back into the seat, catching her mouth in a series of kisses. "Also as far as I'm concerned —" He hissed her deeply again. "— our baby was conceived this morning. It's a honeymoon baby."

She was breathless as his kiss moved over her lips.

Lunch was in one of the upscale, trendy restaurants that Kiley had always wanted to go to. Then Rand surprised her. Instead of dropping her off like she suspected, he stayed with her, taking her to shops she'd never dared go to before.

Kiley found a few things she liked, but when it became apparent that she really wasn't comfortable he took her to a big mall and let her wander. As they browsed, Rand offered his opinion but always let her have the last say, except for insisting she purchase two exquisite evening gowns that she figured she would never need.

It took almost three hours, but they ended up with four pairs of shoes, three skirts, two dresses, two slacks, three jeans and almost a dozen shirts and sweaters, a jacket and a suit that Kiley was also skeptical about needing. Intimate apparel, another nightgown, this one in a soft blue, and a thick, fluffy, white, terrycloth robe like she'd always wanted finished up their clothing purchases. Then they headed to the market for personal items.

Kiley was about exhausted when they finished. "I didn't realize there was so much stuff to basic living."

"Yeah, like hot chocolate in three different flavors and just as many bottles of bubble baths," he teased.

Instead of blushing like he expected, she met his gaze straight on. "Those are my splurges. Everyone is entitled to a weakness or two."

He held up his hands in mock surrender. "I'm all for that as long as you share."

"You want to share my bubble bath?"

As soon as she said it, he got his blush. "Oh, yes!" His wicked look deepened her color.

They stopped at a steak house for dinner so they wouldn't have to cook when they got home, especially since Rand doubted that there was much there to cook.

Darkness had fallen by the time they drove through the neighborhood to his house.

"I've never been to your house before." Kiley sat forward trying to get a better view.

"I'll warn you my house isn't quite finished. You can decorate it however you want."

A few minutes later they pulled up to an old stone fence with a heavy iron-gate. An 'M' figured prominently high above the road. For the first time, Kiley felt a chill run through her at the differences in her and Rand's background.

As if sensing her discomfort, Rand spoke. "It's all right Kiley. This is my family's property. It has been for generations. Someday it will be our children's, but right now it's mine. There are actually four houses on the estate. Vanessa and her lot now occupy the old main house. My mother lives in my parents' house where I grew up. There's a groundskeeper's house and then my house that I built last year. The houses are situated on twenty-seven acres, enough space for you to have your privacy. This is your home. I want you to be comfortable."

Kiley could hear the sincerity in his voice, but it did little to ease the discord inside her. In ways she was thankful for the darkness, which she figured hid most of her strange new world.

The house Rand turned toward was dark, but as they pulled up, security lights came on lighting the yard and four-car garage. The sight of what she saw took her breath away. She didn't get time to comment as the garage door opened and he pulled inside.

The garage was huge and cleaner than any garage Kiley had ever seen. A new SUV was the only other car parked in there, but it could easily hold four more cars. A row of floor-to-ceiling cabinets lined the wall in front. A mountain bike was parked by the door, and on the far wall a canoe rested, attesting to Rand's interest in sports.

Kiley was so busy studying the surroundings she never notice Rand come around the car until he opened the door and scooped her up in his arms. Kiley squealed, throwing her arms around his neck.

"Rand, I can walk."

"It's tradition to carry the bride over the thresh-hold."

"But you did that last night."

"So, I found I like carrying you." He kissed her soundly to forestall any argument.

The kiss broke only long enough for him to give her the number for the keypad lock and the security code inside. He nibbled and nuzzled her neck as she put in the numbers, almost making her mess up. The instant the last number was touched to reactivate the system, he reclaimed her lips. He continued kissing her through the house to his bedroom where he laid her on the bed and followed her down.

For Kiley, her nervousness and wish to explore the house was completely forgotten.

ᏓᏲ

Rand sat at the counter drinking a glass of orange juice and looking out over his backyard. The morning sun glistened off the pool, but it was the large, open area beyond that held his attention. He wondered if Kiley would like a greenhouse built there. As soon as she woke up, he decided to ask her, but for now she needed her rest.

He smiled. Life didn't get much better. He just wished he didn't have to go to work today. Unfortunately, he had an eleven o'clock meeting he couldn't postpone. At least it was late enough for Kiley to sleep-in, so he wouldn't have to wake her to say good-bye.

The knocking on the kitchen door drew his attention. "Good morning." His mother greeted him as he pressed a kiss to her cheek, letting her in.

"Good morning," Rand returned. "What brings you out so early?"

"Trying to catch you. It's been two weeks since I've seen you."

"That's not unusual." Rand got her down a glass for juice.

"True, but the last time you saw me you were on your way to make a baby. You might think that I would be curious on how things turned out. Am I going to be a grandmother? Did your college student, how shall we say, pass her grade?"

"Yes and no," Rand answered cryptically.

"Not funny, darling," his mother chastised.

"All right, let me tell you first you were correct when you talked about not knowing when I would find that someone special."

"You met someone?"

"Yes."

"Is the baby going to be a problem?"

"No."

"Then I'm not about to be a grandmother yet."

"Well actually you are. It's just not the student like I planned." He explained about the accident and then told her about Kiley.

"You fell in love with the girl who is going to have your baby."

"Yes."

"I'm going to be a grandmother," his mother said in awe.

"Correct." He put his arm around her shoulder. "There is one more thing I have to tell you."

"Rand." He heard his name called softly from the family room.

CB80

Kiley was alone when she opened her eyes, but Rand's scent was all around her on the king-sized bed. The pillow beside her still held the indentation from his head. The drapes were pulled, keeping the sun from entering the French doors that Kiley knew lined one wall.

Sliding from the bed, Kiley found the robe they purchased for her yesterday draped across a wing chair with her crutches leaning next to it. She slid on the robe then crossed to the window, pulling opened the drapes to get her first view outside Rand's home. She wasn't surprised at the sight of the swimming pool, but the lavish landscaping did shock her. A myriad of trees and plants surrounded the back of the house. She loved it but couldn't wait to start adding more flowers.

Tearing herself from the view, she stepped into the master bath to freshen up before going to search for Rand. What she found along the way was a mostly empty house. The upstairs was barren except for Rand's room and one other room that held a variety of exercise equipment.

Downstairs, just off the foyer, the living room was also empty. To one side, the den was filled with a large maple desk, leather couch, two matching wing chairs, and a built-in bookcase that was almost completely filled. She knew this was the room where Rand spent his time.

Cutting through the family room, she found it sparsely decorated, dominated by a large flat screen TV, an elaborate sound system, and a huge leather sectional sofa. Kiley started to stop to check his taste in music, but the sound of voices drew her to the kitchen.

"Rand." She pushed open the set of swinging doors. Her stomach dropped at the sight of him with his arm around a beautiful woman. "Excuse me." She started to turn as tears filled her eyes.

"Kiley."

Before she could make it out of the room Rand was there, sliding his arm around her.

"Where you going?" He directed her into the kitchen. "I want you to meet my mother, Elizabeth Monroe. Mother this is Kiley, Kiley Adams Monroe, my wife."

Totally shocked, Kiley fidgeted. Embarrassed, she pulled the lapels of her robe tighter, mindful that she had nothing on underneath.

Elizabeth Monroe had no such hesitations. She came forward putting her arms around Kiley. "Welcome to the family." Her voice was warm and friendly.

"You're married." She looked back at her son. "When?"

"Day before yesterday."

"I should be upset with you, but I'm too happy to be." She turned to Kiley. "So you caught my son. Good for you. I've been hoping for it to happen for a long time. You'll learn soon enough that I'm nosey. I want to hear all about it."

Kiley wasn't sure what to say, she found herself feeling more at ease. Still, she was a little shaky when she excused herself to go upstairs to dress. She was staring at her new wardrobe trying to regain her composure as much as to pick out something to wear when an arm slid around her waist.

"Oh." She jumped and Rand laughed, pulling her back against him, kissing her neck.

"Are you all right?"

"If my heart starts beating again I will be."

He kissed her neck again. "Seriously, you seemed a little – I don't know. I thought you were going to cry there for a moment." When she pulled from him, he knew he was right. "Hey, hey," he turned her back in his arms. "What is it?"

"It's nothing." She glanced away, biting a lip, before turning back. "I'm a little embarrassed, okay."

"Embarrassed about what?"

"Let's see – meeting my new mother-in-law wearing nothing but a robe."

"You don't have anything on under there." His voice drop to a suggestive tone. "Maybe I should check this out." He slid his hand into the material.

"Rand, no." She pulled away. "It's bad enough that I felt jealous over my mother-in-law but I am not going to–"

"You were jealous of my mother." Rand cut her off pulling her back against him, laughing.

"Well, your mom doesn't look that old. She's a very beautiful woman." Kiley's embarrassment reached a new level.

"My mother would thank you for the compliment, and I do have to agree my mother is a beautiful woman and doesn't look her age, but I assure you, the only woman I plan on making love to in the kitchen or any other place is you."

"Rand." she squeaked, batting at his hands. "I'm sorry, it's just all so new, and I'm having trouble believing it really could be real, that you could love me. I really don't fit in your world."

"I think you fit perfectly and I do love you." He gave her a long sensual kiss to prove it. Kiley was still flushed when she returned back downstairs a few minutes later after she'd managed to get dressed.

൦�ep൦

Over the next two days, Kiley took it easy while Rand worked. Her ankle healed enough to get off the crutches, giving her more freedom to investigate the Monroe estate. On the fourth day, a moving van pulled in the driveway. Unsure what was going on, she stepped back as they started to unload boxes in the garage.

It wasn't until they started to unload furniture and remove the packing blankets from around her great-grandmother's sideboard that she realized what all the stuff was. Rand pulled into the driveway a few minutes later to find tears in her eyes as she ran out to throw her arms around his neck.

"Thank you, thank you," she cried over and over against him before she raised her head to press kisses all over his face.

Unable to help it, he broke up laughing. "You're welcome."

"How did you…?"

"I just had a crew go in. They couldn't save everything. The settee and chair will have to be reupholstered because of the smoke damage. There are a lot of boxes that you'll have to go through. They'll be kept in the garage until you do. They could save most of the stuff in the kitchen, dining room and living room and the antique bed set from the first bedroom."

"Thank you," she said again, wiping tears from her face.

"You're welcome, again." He stole another kiss. "Come on, you need to decide where you want everything put in the house. In a day or so, you can go pick out the upholstery material you want. After we get your furniture settled in the house, we can go pick up whatever else you would like to go in the rest of the house."

"I can't believe you did this for me."

"Darling." He wrapped his arms around her. "I'll do anything for you."

"You could get in trouble saying something like that."

"That may be true in most cases, but I know you would never take advantage of me."

"You don't think I can take advantage of you." she challenged, running her finger up his chest then down over his stomach to his waistband. The groan that rumbled in his throat brought a wicked smile to her lips.

"I think maybe I like the idea of you taking advantage of me."

She pressed up against him sliding her arms around his waist. "I guess we'll find out later."

Rand decided he liked this new confidant, playful Kiley. The first time she gave herself to him, she had been shy but there had been a total abandonment that delighted him. There was no doubt that she was giving herself to him. That she was forever his and he was her choice.

As soon as the men drove away, Kiley throw her arms around Rand and gave him a kiss that led to her taking advantage of him without a single complaint. Later, after they ate, Rand told her of the other surprise he had for her. He walked her across the back lawn, arm in arm, as he described the small greenhouse he planned to have built. She was even more shocked and delighted when he told her the construction would start the next day.

# Chapter Ten

Kiley couldn't take her eyes off the workers. For hours they had been at work. First, just two men measuring and staking out the layout, then an hour ago a big truck arrived with a backhoe. As they started to move the dirt around Kiley knew this was not going to be the small greenhouse she'd imagined, but a full, elaborate greenhouse like she never even allowed herself to dream of having.

She could hardly believe Rand would do this for her. That he had realized flowers were not only important to her for a job, but that a love for their beauty and watching them grow gave her enjoyment.

"What is going on here at this unheavenly hour? What are they building?"

"It's a greenhouse." Kiley turned with great enthusiasm toward the woman who had come to stand just behind her. It was obvious, by the scowl on the woman's face, she didn't share her excitement.

The woman was probably about the same age as Rand's mother, in her mid to late fifties. Flaming red hair curved around her perfectly made-up face which held not even an ounce of warmth. An emerald velvet pantsuit hugged her sleek body that was rigid with displeasure. "And why in the world would Rand build a greenhouse when the gardener can order whatever we need?"

"He's doing it for me." Kiley couldn't help but smile at the thought.

The woman drew her gaze over Kiley, taking in her jeans and short sleeved sweater. The look she gave her suggested she found her lacking. "And, who are you?"

"I'm Kiley. You must be Vanessa." Kiley held out her hand determined not to let the woman intimidate her. When the woman failed to acknowledge the gesture, Kiley dropped her hand to her side, tugging on the seam of her pants.

"And why would he build a greenhouse for you here?"

"Because I love flowers, and it will be easier for me here."

"I wasn't told we'd hired a new gardener."

"Oh, I'm not the gardener. I'm Rand's wife." Kiley stressed it, feeling a little need to shock the woman for her rudeness.

"Wife!" Vanessa's gasp was echoed by a male voice that came from behind her.

Kiley spun around to the man who had come up to join them. The tailored, three-piece suit was cut to fit the lean male body to perfection. The pocket-handkerchief matched the lavender tie. His black hair was styled without a single hair out of place. He was almost too handsome.

Maybe that was what left Kiley cold. He was too perfect. His dark eyes slid over her, accessing her curves with an intensity that seemed to strip away her clothes.

Kiley shuddered, resisting the urge to wrap her arms around herself. "Hello." Kiley again stretch out her hand. This time it was accepted and held. Quickly, Kiley tried to remove it, but it was caught tight as long fingers brushed the inside of her wrist.

"Rand has a wife." The words were as smooth as the rest of him. "This is a surprise. I guess this makes me your uncle. I'm Reginald Hammond."

"And when did this happen?" Vanessa bit out.

"Six days ago." Kiley looked back to the woman, breaking her hand free.

Vanessa let out a word that Kiley didn't think she would ever hear out of a lady. "Rand got himself a wife. I presume he has you pregnant, too."

Kiley's breath caught, surprised at the woman's venom. Rand had told her all about the aspects of the will and about Vanessa, but she really hadn't contemplated that the woman might react this way. After all, Rand had said Vanessa had been given a large settlement, and from what Rand said, she had never had any dealings with the company.

"Whether Kiley is pregnant or not has nothing to do with you!"

Kiley had to turn to make sure the voice was Rand's. She had never heard him sound so cold before. He didn't move his eyes from Vanessa as he came up to Kiley, sliding his arm around her, pulling her to him. His body was rigid, muscles taunt, but as she circled her arms around his waist, he softened a bit, molding her to him. When she looked up, he glanced down, a smile crested his lips before he brushed them across her temple.

"Isn't that sweet." Another voice added in, this one sounding sincere.

Kiley turned slightly to see another woman standing to the side. She didn't know how she failed to notice the absolutely stunning, voluptuous woman, but realized she must have been there the whole time.

"Sickening is more like it." Vanessa spat, then turned her attention on Rand. "What do you think you're doing?" She waved her hand at the construction.

"Building a greenhouse for Kiley. She likes to garden."

"You married the gardener. Couldn't you at least marry someone respectable, or was she cheaper to buy off and get pregnant?"

Rand tensed again. "Shut up, Vanessa." He let go of Kiley and stepped forward.

"How dare you tell me to shut up," the woman shrieked. "You think you've won. I'm sure a tramp wasn't what Conrad meant, and you will have to prove the baby is yours. Can you be certain?"

"You vicious …" Kiley had never seen Rand so furious. Obviously, neither had the others as they started to retreat as he approached. "Let me make this clear. You will never, never insult Kiley again. She is sweet, honest and has more integrity and true beauty than you have fake haughtiness. Kiley never would trick me or use me, and I have tried to be just as honest with her."

Outrage boiled from him. "I married Kiley because I love her and any child born will be mine, and I will love it. And though, you have absolutely no need to know this, so there will not be any misunderstanding, Kiley was a virgin on our wedding night. You will treat her with respect. Is that understood?"

He stared them down a minute while getting himself in check. "Now, if you will excuse me, it is almost noon on a beautiful day. I have finished my work for the day and have come to take my wife to lunch and spent the rest of the day with her." He turned, sliding his arm around Kiley, drawing her away with him, leaving the trio behind and the men still working three hundred feet away.

They didn't quite make it back to the house when Rand suddenly stopped. Turning her in his arms, he took possession of her mouth savagely, drinking her in as his hand raced over her body, molding her into him. Shudders of released tension wracked his body, quickly changing to tension of another type as she trembled in return. He tried to break away, but it still took several minutes before he managed enough control to pull back.

"I'm sorry." He rested his forehead against hers.

"I'm not." Her words were breathless as she clung to him.

"I didn't mean the kiss." He ducked to brush his lips against hers. "I meant about my step-grandmother and her offspring. I didn't want you to have to meet them on your own, and I shouldn't have blurted out your innocence to them."

Kiley shook her head and pressed her body back to his. "It doesn't matter. Just kiss me again." She caught his bottom lip between her teeth.

Rand groaned complying with her wish. "Sweetheart," he said speaking into her mouth. "We keep this up and we'll never make it to the bedroom."

"I've never made love outside."

"I'm aware of that, but there are too many people around for you to do it now." He tugged her toward the house. They still never made it to the bedroom. Instead, Kiley got her first experience at making love in the kitchen. Once in their bedroom, it was another hour before they got ready to go to lunch.

∽୧୦∾

Sunday afternoon, they attended a party that his mother pulled together to start to introduce Kiley around. Many of the area's most influential people were there, but Kiley was most interested in meeting Rand's friends. Rand explained that he didn't have many close friends because he spent too much time on business.

His closest friend was the new assistant district attorney, Ryan Buchanan. They had been friends growing up. Even going to different universities hadn't disrupted their friendship. Kiley found she immediately liked the dark haired man, who was a little leaner and two inches taller than Rand.

"This man was a killer at the net." Rand told Kiley, his arm wrapped tight around her as the three talked.

"Basketball?" Kiley questioned.

"Volleyball. We still play when we can," Ryan answered. "Looks like you're playing days will be cut down though, old boy."

"Why?" Kiley asked. "I love to watch volleyball. I even played in high school. I thought of going out for it in college but things didn't work out."

Rand knew it was because of her grandfather's death, but Kiley didn't dwell on it.

She shrugged. "I probably wouldn't have made it, though. I was a little short to be much of a threat at the net. My spikes were passable at best. Digs and setting were my specialty."

"All right, we can always use a good setter. Nice move man." Ryan slapped Rand on the shoulder.

"Honestly, this is one of her good points I didn't know about."

"You mean she has others," Ryan quipped.

"Oh yeah," Rand smiled down at her, taking the chance to sneak a kiss.

"Newlyweds." Ryan rolled his eyes.

"Better be careful. Someday it will be your turn," Rand said.

"Maybe, if I can find a woman like Kiley. Anymore like her at home?"

"Nope, she's an original and all mine," Rand said with a teasing smugness.

"Some guys have all the luck."

"I agree." The look Rand gave Kiley left her with no doubt he truly meant it.

After another couple of minutes, Kiley excused herself to let them talk while she went outside for a breath of fresh air. She walked out over the lawn, enjoying the smell of the freshly mowed lawn and the flowering trees.

She'd already had the opportunity to meet the full-time gardener. Mr. Myer was an older, widowed man who loved plants as much as Kiley and was enthused to help her with the greenhouse. She knew Rand was happy with his reaction to Kiley and figured he'd found someone else to help watch out for her. Kiley suspected Rand was right. Mr. Myer already treated her like one of his daughters he'd told her so much about. Kiley smiled to herself, thinking of the man.

"Hi."

Kiley turned, startled. "Hi," she greeted the sexy woman who'd been at the greenhouse. As she watched the woman shifted almost like she was timid, which seemed at odds with how low-cut her mini dress was and incredibly high her spiked heels.

"I never got to talk to you the other day. I'm Veronica Hammond, but you can call me Ronnie. I guess you can say, I'm Rand's step-aunt. It's something like that. It so funny because he's older that me." She glanced down then up. "Are you really married to Rand?"

Kiley immediately got the impression that the woman wasn't trying to be rude. She was just a ... air head. "Yes."

"Wow, you eloped, that is so spectacular."

Kiley was surprised at her choice of words, she was even more surprised when the woman moved close and asked softly. "Is it true you were a virgin?"

Kiley had to swallow to keep from choking or laughing at Ronnie's expression. "Yes," she answered clearly.

"Wow, I mean well, wow, and Rand is such a hunk. I can't believe he would wait."

This time Kiley did laugh.

"I said something wrong, didn't I?" Ronnie looked distressed. "I always say the wrong thing. Mother and Eloise always tell me to keep my mouth shut. They said the only way I'd ever get a man was with my body, but Rand married you before you slept together. I like Rand. I wish he would have paid attention to me, but mother, Eloise and Reggie, well…" She shrugged.

Kiley sensed deep inside Ronnie there was a genuine person who was lonely and had been suppressed by her mother and siblings for a long time. Kiley just wasn't sure how to approach her. Ronnie took care of that.

"I like plants. I have some violets in my room. They like the morning light."

"That's right. They were my grandmother's favorite flower." Kiley was just getting comfortable with the woman when they were interrupted.

"Isn't this quaint." From the sound of the voice, Kiley expected to find Vanessa, instead a much younger woman walked toward them. She was probably only a half a dozen years older than Ronnie. Though, there wasn't any resemblance between the sisters, it had to be Eloise,

"Eloise, this is Kiley." Ronnie confirmed he guess. "She's Rand's wife."

"Broodmare would be a more apt a description. Mother's looking for you." The stern tone left no doubt Eloise was not pleased with her sister. The smile dropped from Ronnie's face as she turned from Kiley.

"I'll talk to you later, Ronnie," Kiley said.

When Ronnie looked back as if to say something Eloise cut her off. "Mother will not want to wait."

Kiley aptly interpreted it as their mother wouldn't approve of Ronnie's association with her. Kiley sadly watched Ronnie walk away.

"So you're Rand's new plaything. When are you going to have a baby? You do know that is why Rand married you."

"I know about the will, if that's what you mean."

"Rand told you." There was a moment of shock on her face then it slipped to a smirk. "Yes, of course he would. I'm sure he offered you a fair compensation, too."

"I'd say so, he gave me his love." Kiley moved to go around her. "If you'll excuse me, I think I'll go find my husband."

Rand was in the middle of a conversation with a group of people. When she stepped next to him, his arm came out around her waist, pulling her close, though he didn't look toward her. Kiley slid her arms around his waist, giving him a squeeze. Rand glanced down at her, giving her a private smile. She thought he would look away, but instead he turned to her, brushing his lips against her temple, before turning back to the group as he introduced Kiley.

A short time later, Kiley was again on her own when another member of Rand's extended family approached her. Reggie caught her moving around the room and asked her to dance. Kiley glanced at the few couples actually dancing and tried to decline as the man took a hold of her. When she stepped back, he followed.

"I don't think so," she said, taking another step back.

"Come on now. I have a business proposition for you."

"Oh."

"Yes. You see, I'll give you double what Rand is giving you not to get pregnant."

"What?" She was shocked by his bluntness.

"I said double." The man stepped forward, trapping her back against the wall. "Whatever Rand offered you."

"I don't think that's possible, even if I were interested."

"Oh, we can pay, just name you price."

"Rand offered me his love, and that's all I want."

"The only love Rand has is for Roe Technologies."

"You're wrong, and you have nothing that could tempt me away from him."

Without warning, the man clasped her hand and pulled her toward him. To anyone watching, it would look like they were dancing, but Kiley struggled to break free from the surprisingly strong hold.

"I'm sure you don't want to cause a scene," Reginald's voice rasped in her ear. "But I'll warn you not to let Rand get you pregnant and don't get involved with our family's business."

Kiley pulled away glaring into the Reginald's cold, dark eyes, but before anything could happen, she felt a hand on her elbow and Rand's voice tickle across her ear.

"Mind if I cut in? I haven't had a chance to dance with my beautiful wife, yet."

Before Reginald could object, Rand turned Kiley's stiff body, and danced her away. After a moment, he felt a tremor run though her body, and she sagged into him. Instinctively, he tightened his hold, running his fingers over her neck. "Are you all right?" he whispered in her ear.

She nodded, burying her face into his shoulder. Another shiver shook her body countering the nod. Rand pulled back slightly, raising a hand to her face to tilt it up. "What's wrong?"

When she took too long a time finding her voice, he jumped in with the answer. "He threatened you." Rage filled his face, and Rand shifted to search the crowd.

"Rand, please, it's all right." Kiley's hand came up to stroke his face, soothing away the anger that spiked in his body.

He turned back, running his fingers across her cheek, caressing the softness in return. His touch restored her composure. "He offered to pay me not to get pregnant."

"You didn't tell him you were?" There was huskiness in his voice.

"No, he doesn't deserve to know." She kissed his fingers.

Rand nodded. "Well, we'll keep it private as long as we can. Speaking of the baby, I came looking for you because there's someone here I thought that you might like to see. That was before I decided to keep you for myself long enough to dance. Come on." He led her into the other room where Dr. Matthews stood with his wife, an elegant, matronly woman. They were the first people Kiley knew other than Rand's family.

"Dr. Matthews, Mrs. Matthews," Kiley exclaimed seeing the couple."

"There you are dear," Dr. Matthews greeted her.

Kiley got a warm hug from the older couple.

"You look wonderful." Mrs. Matthews smiled. "I could hardly believe it when I heard you'd run off and gotten married, but you look happy."

"I am." Kiley knew she was beaming but didn't care.

"Congratulations," the older couple said together. They hugged Kiley again, shaking hands with Rand.

"Can I get you a drink?" Rand offered.

"Just water please," Laura Matthews said as her husband shook his head.

"Same." Kiley added and he left to get them.

"You do look happy," Mrs. Matthews commented.

"I really am."

"Good," Dr. Matthews said as he escorted the women over to a couple empty chairs. "I was extremely concerned about what happened to you, but it looks to have worked out. Rand is a good man. I have known his mother for years."

"He is wonderful. I still have trouble believing this is not a dream."

"You've fallen in love with him," Mrs. Matthews observed with great pleasure.

Kiley blushed slightly. "Yes." She received another hug.

"Your grandmother would be so pleased. She was worried you gave up so much for her. She'd be tickled. It's too bad about your house, though. Milton called me after Rand called about you. We drove by – it's just lucky you're all right."

"I haven't been by since the first day. Rand had a crew salvage as much as possible. I'm going over there tomorrow to check it out and see about my floral supplies in the garage."

Kiley thought about the night before when she had told Rand her plans of going to the house. It had almost been their first argument since their marriage. Rand didn't like the thought of her picking up her little car from the repair shop where it had been for almost two weeks and then going to her house alone. He wanted her to wait until he could go with her.

He also objected about her car, wanting her to take the SUV. When she said she didn't want something so big, he suggested that she take his car. He even told her he would buy her a new car, any kind she wanted as long as it had a good safety rating and was dependable. Her statement that she was a safe driver and had never even had a ticket didn't appease him, but she held firm.

It was when she kissed him and told him it was really sweet that he wanted to protect her, and she loved him that the debate was forgotten and so was everything else for a while. She smiled to herself, continuing her visit with the Matthews.

# Chapter Eleven

It was mid-morning when the taxi dropped Kiley off at the auto shop, where she picked up her car and drove to her house. Pulling into the driveway, she waved to Mr. Jacobs, the elderly man who lived on the corner.

The house didn't look that much different than the last time she saw it. Yellow police tape still circled the yard. Heavy plastic fluttered and plywood was boarded up over the burned area.

A tear slipped free. Kiley wiped it away as she got out of the car. The house looked so sad and desolate. She didn't try to enter, though she did stop to look in the windows. The empty rooms seemed so barren and forlorn, not at all like the home she remembered. Still, the crew Rand hired did a good job cleaning out the house.

As she made her way around the yard, it was obvious that between the storm and the firemen, little could be salvaged from her gardens. She consoled herself that later she might be able to get some plant starts for her greenhouse and gardens. She felt a little more pain at the loss of her house lessen when she realized that she was beginning to think of Rand's house as her home.

In a better mood, she made her way to the garage, which remained untouched. Pulling open the wide doors, she was greeted by the sweet floral scent of drying flowers which hung from the rafters and were stacked on shelves along the wall with her other supplies. Her two large worktables took most of the floor space. Next to the table sat her stool. Everything was as if she'd just left it, though it felt like an eternity.

Seeing no need to hurry, she sat down to add the finishing touches to the three arrangements she had in progress, figuring she'd call the shops when she got home. Then she could deliver them with the other three swags she had waiting on the shelf. She had called the shops after the fire. They were very understanding about her delay. She hoped that would continue until she could restock her supplies. For the first little while, she would have to buy the flowers, but she would do her best to keep her good reputation.

Her focus was on the flowers she needed when she locked up and headed for home, wanting to be there in time to fix dinner for Rand. As she merged onto the freeway, her thoughts turned to dinner and the enjoyment she had sharing meals with him.

Kiley didn't notice the car crowding her until she approached her exit. She saw the car just before it bumped the back of her car. Terror filled her heart, but she tried to remain calm. Pressing the accelerator, she pulled ahead and signaled to change lanes. As soon as she moved, another car came up on her right.

When she looked back at the left-hand lane, the first car pulled up beside her car, locking her in. Kiley hit her horn hoping to get the person's attention, fear rising as the car on the right bumped her again. A cry escaped her when the car on the left returned the bump.

The sound of metal crunching filled her small car. Kiley fought for control. Removing her foot from the gas-peddle, Kiley resisted the urge to slam on the brakes and pressed down lightly.

The car on the left slammed into her again. Kiley screamed, struggling with the wheel as the car pulled alongside. Kiley glanced at the other car and felt another stab of horror at the sight of the ski mask-covered face.

Her attention was still diverted when the other car hit her again from behind. The steering wheel jerked in her hands as the tail end of her car was clipped again. Even with the slowed momentum, her car began to slide.

The world spun in nauseating circles. The seatbelt bit into her shoulder as she was thrown to the side. The car jolted off the road, bumped then rocked, coming to a stop against the drainage ditch that ran down the middle of the highways.

Stunned, Kiley sat still as the dust dissipated around her. The white airbag lay limp in her lap. She had no recollection of it going off. Beside her, metal groaned as the door was wedged open the few possible inches.

"Sit still," a male voice commanded beside her. "The highway patrol and ambulance are on the way." The male voice kept talking to her until the siren drowned him out.

The other side door was opened, and a man in uniform crawled in next to her. Kiley assured the EMT she was all right except for a headache and some nausea that could be because she was pregnant and hadn't eaten in a while.

Still, he checked her over, placing a collar on her neck. "Just a precaution," he assured her when tears filled her eyes. "It will be a few minutes before we get you out of the car."

Kiley didn't care how long it was. She just wanted Rand.

"My … my purse." The words wobbled out.

"It will be taken care of."

She went to shake her head and couldn't. "Phone's in it. Please, can I call my husband?"

"We normally…" he started then reached into the purse by his knee and punched the speed dial for her.

Kiley had only talked to Beth, Rand's secretary, once. When Kiley asked for him, the woman started to say he was in a meeting, then stopped. Whether she detected the tremor in Kiley's voice or Rand had left instructions, the woman told her to hold on while she got Rand.

It felt like forever, but it was only about twenty seconds before Kiley heard him say her name.

"Rand," she cried trying to stop the tears when he called her name again in panic. "I'm all … I'm … someone ran me off the road."

"Where are you?" The sound of heavy footfalls came over the phone, and she realized he was running down stairs. He was coming. She felt a strong sense of calm fill her as she described what happened and where she was.

There was a moment break when she guessed he was getting in the car then he was back and asked to speak to the patrolman. She heard the man assure him her condition seemed fine then he mentioned Detective Gerome before handing the phone back to her.

Kiley clung to the phone and Rand's voice as they got her out of the wrecked car and onto the stretcher. They were just strapping her down when Rand arrived. Trying to stay out of the way, he caught her hand.

"Rand."

He only got to hold her a few seconds before he was forced back. It gave him a moment to look around. His heart hadn't been normal since he'd first heard Kiley's frightened voice on the phone, and seeing her car didn't do anything to ease its pounding. Now that she was out.

The car sat abandoned. Both doors hung open, the driver's side crumpled. The body was a horrifying mass of dents. Feeling the need to be close to Kiley, he moved to her feet, sliding a hand along her ankle.

"Rand?" Her voice still was not steady.

"Right here baby." He moved up a little so she could see him.

"Do you think the baby's all right?"

He winced, thinking of the endearment he'd just used.

"The doctor will check you over and make sure, but as tough as you are this little accident was nothing, just an excuse for me to buy you a new car."

"Determined to win are you."

"Yeah, start thinking of the color."

"Rand, I feel sick."

"It'll be all right, sweetheart." He stroked his hand up and down her leg. "I've already called Dr. Matthews' office. He should be waiting when they get you to the hospital."

Rand was right. Dr. Matthews was waiting when the ambulance pulled up to the emergency. With a quick assurance to Rand, he accompanied Kiley into the examination room leaving Rand to do the paperwork and pace the floor.

For Rand time passed agonizingly slow. Papers done, he stepped outside long enough to call his secretary to arrange for his car to be picked up from along the highway and delivered to the hospital. He'd been in the emergency room about an hour when Gerome arrived. His brief account of the witness reports sent chills up Rand's spine.

"It was obvious there were two attackers, working together, but they fled after she went off the road. Unfortunately, we didn't get a good description on either car. Everyone was more concerned about her than getting details. The big question is, are they partners or just hired help?" Gerome said.

"Reggie threatened Kiley." Rand said then explained what happened at the party.

"Okay. Since I can't talk with your wife yet, I'll go have a chat with him. See what other information might have come up, then I'll get back with you." With that Gerome left.

Rand tried to settle in a chair then gave up and paced the waiting room, finally coming to rest leaning against the wall. He studied the people huddled in the room. Each showed concern and fear for their loved ones. It was the same, male to female; toddler to aged. Some dressed in tattered clothes, some casual and some in expensive business attire, yet they all had a common bond in that room. For some the news would be good, for others devastating, which he knew, if Kiley lost the baby, it would be for him. Not because of some foolish will, but because he loved Kiley, and they loved the baby she carried.

Most men loved their baby because it was conceived of love. This baby brought him Kiley. It gave him his love. All the money in the world meant nothing next to it.

He closed his eyes fighting back the tears. When he opened them again Dr. Matthews was walking toward him. Rand pushed away from the wall, but couldn't say anything.

Dr. Matthews seemed to understand, greeting him with, "Kiley will be fine. She has a concussion, so is having some nausea. I put three stitches in her forehead where she bumped it on the car door, but the x-ray is clear."

"Thank you." Rand got out. "The baby?" He was almost afraid to ask.

"It appears just fine, also. No bleeding, no cramping. We ran an ultrasound, and the uterus looks good, no sign of tearing. Of course, the baby is still too small to see any problems. I'm admitting her for the night for observation, just to be cautious with the baby and the concussion. I also want her to stay down for a couple days because she has had so many traumas lately, but Kiley's young and strong. I don't foresee any problems."

Rand ran his fingers back through his hair. "Thank you again."

"You're welcome. I have to get back to the office. Tell Kiley I'll see her in the morning. They're moving her to the third floor. You can stop at the nurses' desk for the room number."

Rand headed up the stairs not wanting to wait for the elevator. They were just getting Kiley settled when he arrived. She looked pale against the white pillow, but smiled when she saw him.

"Did you see Dr. Matthews?" she asked anxiously.

Rand nodded forcing a smile. "He said you were fine. Good thing you have a hard head." He leaned down and kissed her forehead on the opposite side from the bandage that covered her stitches. "How do you feel?"

"I still feel sick to my stomach, and I'm sleepy."

"I'm afraid that's par for the course. They won't let you sleep much for the next twenty-four hours, but look at the bright side."

"What's that?"

He raised his eyebrows suggestively. "You have me to keep you company." He settled in the chair next to the bed, taking her hand.

The next day, Rand was allowed to take her home. About noon Detective Gerome stopped by to get her statement.

She went over everything, but since the person she saw was wearing a ski mask she couldn't even tell him if it was a man or a woman. "I'm sorry, I'm no help." She blew out a breath. She gave Rand a weak smile when he gave her hand a light squeeze.

"It's all right," Gerome soothed. "We know one of the cars was stolen from a front yard in a quiet neighborhood. The keys had been left in it. It was found abandoned at the mall. No prints."

"Kind of figures," Rand said in frustration.

"Yeah well, we still have nothing on the other vehicle, so there's still a chance." Gerome went for a positive.

Kiley couldn't add anything else to help, so after Gerome's assurance that he'd keep checking, the detective left.

"I think it is time for you to rest," Rand said, after seeing the detective to the door.

"I'm fine, really."

The words hardly made it out of her mouth before Rand picked her up and carried her to bed, then to quiet her, he laid down beside her until she fell asleep.

The next day, Rand had to go to the office and insisted that Kiley go with him. Kiley was amazed to find he had several framed pictures of them already there. On his desk was a picture from her house that had been taken about a year ago by her grandmother, who had captured Kiley working in her garden, surrounded by flowers. There was also the picture of their wedding kiss. Rand had brought the same print home and put on their dresser as a surprise.

Rand was a surprise. In business she knew he was powerful, but to her, he was a romantic, always looking for ways to please her. She felt a rush of warmth as she settled down to read while he attended his meetings. After a while, she decided she was tired and moved to the leather couch to nap.

When she woke up, she found Rand's suit coat draped over her. He worked quietly at his desk. She watched him for a few minutes before he lifted his head and noticed her open eyes. With an intent look that made her heart race, he rose and came around the large maple desk and crossed the floor. Without a word, he stretched out next to her working his arms around her as he took possession of her lips. His kisses became hungered.

"Rand someone could come in," Kiley protested weakly as she slid her arms around his neck.

"Not a chance." His lips made their way down her neck. "I locked the door and told Beth I didn't want to be disturbed. That you were sleeping."

"I'm not sleeping now," she pointed out.

"And I definitely don't want to be disturbed."

Sometime later, they lay pressed together, utterly content. "I have been dreaming of making love to you on this couch for the last couple hours." He pressed his lips to her temple. "Now I may have to get rid of it because every time I look at it I'll think of you. I'll never be able to get any work done."

Kiley laughed. Blushing, she pressed several kisses along his shoulder. "I may have to come to work with you more often."

"Anytime you want."

Two days later, the police still had no further leads. They did turn up that Reggie had financial problems, with a large gambling debt that he was being pressured to make good on, but he had a solid alibi for when the cars had run her off the road. He also denied knowing anything about Kiley before Saturday.

Rand was feeling frustrated about being helpless to protect her, and Kiley was feeling stressed at her lack of freedom, but to ease his worry, agreed not to leave the house. So she started working on the boxes of her belongings in the garage. She was careful to follow the doctor's direction about no heavy lifting and still made pretty good progress.

She experienced several teary moments finding special things she was afraid were lost and things she didn't even know existed, like a book of genealogy and history of her grandfather's family. Luckily, most of the photos had been in the bottom of the sideboard in the dining room and hadn't been damaged.

She was going through an old album when Rand's mother stopped by. Kiley found she now felt comfortable with Elizabeth Monroe, who seemed to accept her as a daughter, not just a daughter-in-law. They sat together while Kiley showed her pictures and told about her family.

After she left, Kiley laid down for a nap. That was one of the doctor's orders she found no trouble following because, while she wasn't having hardly any morning sickness, she was always sleepy.

The next day, she was surprised when the doorbell rang, and she opened the door to find Ronnie standing there with a sickly looking violet.

"I hope I'm not bothering you?" The woman shifted nervously.

"Not at all," Kiley opened the door wider directing her in. "I was just making cookies."

"You make cookies?" Ronnie said, as if it was the most amazing thing in the world to do.

"Sure. Do you mind if we go in the kitchen?" Kiley led the way.

"I've never been in Rand's house before. There isn't much furniture is there?" She looked around.

"I haven't had much chance to look for any yet."

"I heard about your accident. The police talked to all of us. Reggie was all in a fit because they took him in for questioning."

"I'm sorry."

"It's okay. It must have been scary, being in the car and having someone hit into you."

"It was."

"I'm glad you're okay?"

"Thanks. Do you want to help me with the cookies?"

"I've never made cookies before." There was a hesitation in her voice, but a longing in her eyes.

"There's always a first time, then. Let me get you an apron."

"Mother would be aghast to be caught in the kitchen other than to give orders," Ronnie said as she put a chocolate Hershey Kiss on top of a peanut-butter cookie with the care of handling a masterpiece.

Kiley smiled. "Some of my earliest memories are of making cookies and other things with my mother and grandmother," she said, putting the last pan of cookies in the oven. "Would you like some hot chocolate or juice?"

"I haven't had hot chocolate for a long time."

"Then hot chocolate it is."

"You don't have to make it special."

"No problem. I make it all the time. Rand teases me about being addicted to it. Though, I think he likes it as much or more then I do."

"That seems funny, a grown man, drinking hot chocolate. I mean…" Ronnie shrugged embarrassed. "What I came for was to ask you advice on my flower. It's not doing well. I've only had it a month."

"When the cookies are out, we'll try repotting it and I found fertilizer in a box yesterday that should help."

When they came back in from potting the violet, Ronnie sat on a stool and watched with interest as Kiley started to fix dinner.

"I'm not that big of a slut. Not really. Not like everyone thinks," Ronnie said out of the blue.

Kiley about dropped the spatula but didn't say anything as Ronnie continued. "I haven't slept with that many guys. I only sleep with them if I think they could be the one. I'm just not sure how to figure out who's the right one. They all have said they want me, but they never stay around."

"Ronnie, I'm not sure I'm the one to give you advice on this. My experience is very limited. With my grandmother sick, I didn't date too much. Before that, I had a few crushes and that, but I've only been in love with one man that I could ever think of giving myself to."

"You mean Rand." Ronnie said dreamily.

Kiley smiled shyly and nodded. "I think I fell in love the first moment I saw him. I hit him on the head with a door, and when I looked up at him, I couldn't think or breathe. I never thought that I would see him again, but I couldn't get him out of my mind. Then when we met again it was a … mess, and he was bossy and so wonderful. Anyway, I'm getting off track. I think the trick is not finding a man who wants you. You're so lovely every man will want you. The trick is finding a man who loves you."

"And Rand loves you."

Kiley paused for a moment then smiled deeply." Yes. Yes, I truly believe he does. I don't know why, but I am so thankful."

"I think that's great. I really like you, Kiley."

"I like you, too. I think we'll be great friends."

"My family won't like that, but you know what, I don't care. They never approve of me anyway."

"Well, you can hang out here whenever you want. Are you sure you don't want to stay and join us, Rand wouldn't mind."

"No, I better not, but thank you." She held up the flower.

"You're welcome."

She saw the woman hesitate, "Kiley, you're sure you don't mind if I come back?"

"I'd love it, anytime. As I said, friends."

"Thanks." Ronnie brightened. "I'll see you."

"Homemade cookies," Rand exclaimed, walking into the house a few minutes later. He snitched one and took a bite. "Mmm, I knew marrying you was a wonderful idea." He took another bite. "Come here, my incredible wife, and I'll share."

He gave her a bite then followed it with his mouth. "Sharing is good," he said against her mouth. "I love you," he murmured taking another kiss, then grabbed another cookie. "Mmm," he murmured with satisfaction again. "I didn't even know I had any pans."

"You didn't," Kiley answered. "I found them in a box yesterday. Your kitchen is now completely stocked, and I still have two boxes of stuff for charity."

"Our kitchen." He kissed the end of her nose. "You've been busy, but you're supposed to be taking it easy."

"I am careful, and I took a nap today."

"Good." He wrapped his arms around her, shocking her with his almost incessant need to touch her.

"You must have had a good day."

"Yeah, the best part was coming home to you." He ran kisses along her cheek. "I didn't know how much I was missing. How was your day?"

"Wonderful. Ronnie came to visit."

He stopped, his lips against her neck and pulled back. "You're kidding."

"No, she helped me make cookies. You know, her mom never did that with her growing up."

"No, I doubt she ever did."

"I think that's sad. Did you make cookies with your mom?" She looked concerned.

"Yes," he assured her. "I take it you're going to make cookies with our children."

"Yes, and play games and go for walks."

"Our kids are going to be the luckiest children in the world to have you for a mom."

"Thank you. Rand, how many children would you like?"

He was quiet a second. "I don't know. I was hoping maybe we'd have at least a couple. I always wanted to have a brother or sister."

"I didn't like being an only child, either. I always dreamed of having three or four babies."

"Sounds wonderful to me, but it'll be up to you. You're the one that has to go through carrying them. I just get to have the fun." He twitched his eyebrows in a playful way she was becoming familiar with. "While we're on the subject of children, did my mother mention the children's charity fundraiser on Friday?"

"Yes."

"Feel up to going?"

"Yes." Her voice didn't sound too steady at the thought.

"We don't have to go."

"No, I'd like to go … I just … have never gone to anything like that before."

"You —" he gave her a quick kiss, "—don't need to worry. I will take care of you. This is the one fundraiser I always attend. Partly because my mother has been active with it for about the last eight years, but mainly because I think it's a very worthy cause."

"You're a softy."

"Softy, huh." He swung her around and up into his arms.

# Chapter Twelve

Friday night, dressed in one of the evening gowns Rand had insisted on buying, Kiley stepped into her first charity ball. "What do you think?" Rand leaned over and whispered in her ear.

"There are a lot of people." Her comment brought a laugh from him.

"Let's go find someone you know before we get seated," Rand suggested, leading her around the room. They stopped several times for Rand to introduce her to people and talk a minute before moving on until they met up with Dr. and Mrs. Matthews.

"Oh, you look so lovely. Elcie would have loved to see you all dressed up like this, so beautiful and happy," Mrs. Matthews greeted. "You really are radiant."

"Thank you," Kiley said, feeling a little teary, then talked freely with the couple as they found a table to sit together.

Once dinner was over, the speaker was introduced. While he talked about the infants and children the money would help, one of Kiley's hands found its way into Rand's. She couldn't keep the other from settling over her still-flat abdomen where new life grew.

Rand looked over. When he saw the protective motion of her hand he smiled, and brought the hand he held to his lips, leaving her no doubt of his feelings for the baby she was carrying. Its importance to him was not due to the will.

After the speaker finished, dancing began. Kiley was happy to step into Rand's arms. She marveled at how incredible he looked in a tux, but it made her even happier that their wedding hadn't been formal but just for them. Otherwise it might have been a lot like this ball, with a room full of people, and she would have only known half a dozen of them.

Kiley got used to getting as many looks from women as men. She could understand their interest in Rand. It was hard not to stare at him, but she found that several stares bothered her. Vanessa, Eloise, and Reggie did nothing to hide the contempt in their eyes, but the worst feeling was from the other doctor that had been in Dr. Matthews's office the day she found out she was pregnant. The man's eyes were cold and accusing as they followed her. She was glad when Rand turned her on the dance floor so she no longer had to look at him. She didn't want anything to spoil the perfect night it had been.

It was quite late when the first people began to leave, though there was still at least another hour or two to the party.

"Are you ready to go?" Rand asked.

Kiley was about to assure him that she was fine when she noticed the signs of tiredness around his eyes and nodded.

A few minutes later, they stepped out on the granite steps. Rand asked the valet to retrieve his car. He turned to her while waiting, sliding his arms around her waist. "Well, Mrs. Monroe, how did you like you first big charity ball?"

"It was wonderful. I enjoyed it." She stretched up to give him a quick kiss that lasted a lot longer then she had planned.

At the feel of Kiley in his arms, some of the tiredness fled Rand's body. She was so loving, he knew the feeling she raised in him would never fade and looked forward to the next fifty or so years.

"Good, did I tell you how beautiful you look tonight?"

"Several times."

"Well, I'm saying it again – you look beautiful. You look great in that dress, and I just can't wait to get you home and out of it."

As if on cue, their car pulled up to the curb. While the valet held the door, Rand helped Kiley into the seat. She might not have had a lot of experience in an evening gown, but her natural grace made it look awful good. Slipping the valet a tip, he headed around the car humming. Any man who looked at Kiley would think he was a lucky devil, and they would be right.

Rand had just reached the open door when he heard an engine roar. He turned as headlights flared, blinding him with high beams. Rand stood for a second before his mind registered that the car was headed directly at him. Diving over the trunk of the car, he heard the crunching, tearing of metal, and screaming as he hit the ground and rolled.

The next thing he knew, Kiley was crying his name, running her hands over him. He pushed himself up, as Kiley tried to urge him back down.

"Don't move. You should stay still." Her voice was shaky.

He caught her hand and held it to his chest while making it to a sitting position. "It's all right. I'm fine." He reached up and wiped a tear from her cheek, wincing as he did. "Shh, there is not a mark on me that would wash off or fade in a couple days," he assured her with a calmness that was in direct contradiction to what he was feeling inside.

"Rand." Her arms went around him. She buried her face into his neck and sobbed.

"The police and an ambulance are on their way," the valet said over Kiley's shoulder.

"Thank you, but the ambulance isn't necessary." Rand stroked Kiley's back reassuringly. "Can you go inside and locate Dr. Milton Matthews?" Rand was feeling a little shaky, but what worried him was how upset Kiley was. The valet nodded, making his way through the crowd that had gathered.

Kiley managed a deep unsteady breath and leaned back. Her eyes darted over him. A trembling finger came up to caress his cheek, stopping short of where it stung. Without comment, she took the handkerchief from his pocket and gently wiped away a trail of blood from a small cut that Rand didn't realize was there.

In the distance sirens screamed, but Kiley and Rand remained focused only on each other. Rand caught her fingers, turning them over and bringing them to his lips. Kiley leaned forward pressing her cheek against his undamaged one. Around them flashes burst from photographers' cameras, but neither cared. They said their love without a single word.

It was the police officer asking if he was all right that finally broke them up. Rand made it slowly to his feet, amid assurance that he was. He then helped Kiley rise.

She brushed her hands over his shoulder. "I think you'll need a new tux." The sleeve was ripped and there was a hole in his knee, but Rand's attention focused on the car.

"I think we're both going to need new cars."

The side of the car was smashed in, and the door lay twisted up over the hood. Glass was scattered over the ground and driver's seat. He reached for Kiley, realizing she had been sitting in the car the whole time.

"You're not hurt?" His eyes swept over her.

"No. We're lucky."

"Maybe more so then we think." He nodded down the road. Across the parking lot, about two hundred feet away between a white car and a tree, an officer leaned into the dented, abandoned car that had barely missed Rand. The car matched the description of one of the cars that had forced Kiley off the road.

The officer next to them asked several more questions, then sent the ambulance away empty before returning to them for statements. Detective Gerome showed up as they were going over everything a second time.

"Aren't you ever off duty?" Rand greeted the man as he came forward.

"With you two around?" He looked over at the car and shook his head. "I'd hate to have your insurance rates."

"I imagine they just doubled."

"This time I'd say our guy changed directions."

Rand got his meaning, but didn't want Kiley to think much about it. "Excuse me a moment. There's Dr. Matthews I wanted him to check over Kiley."

"Me? You're the one that was hurt."

"You were a little shaken up. Don't worry. I'll have him take a look at me after I get done talking to Detective Gerome," he said as he directed her toward the Matthews, leaving her in their hands to care for before returning to Gerome.

"Sorry, I wanted her away from this," Rand said, coming back to the officer.

"I understand. As I was going to say, you were the definite target. That does add to the puzzle. Would you like to walk with me to check out the car?"

Rand nodded glancing back to make sure Kiley was all right with the Matthews. Mrs. Matthews had an arm around Kiley's shoulder like a mother hen protecting her young.

"Do you recognize the car?" Gerome asked as they drew near.

"No, I didn't even get a good look at it when it was headed toward me."

"According to witnesses, the driver disappeared into the trees. We're checking the area, but I'm not counting on finding him. We'll run a complete check on the car. We're sure to turn up something. All the alibis check out on your step-family. I'll tell you, your step-grandmother was not happy when we talked to her."

"I can imagine."

"Any idea where they were tonight?"

Rand nodded his head toward the building. "Here at the fund raiser. Veronica was the only one we talked to. The others did a pretty good job of snubbing us."

"Well, I'll still talk to them. Being here would be convenient to keep an eye on you and let someone know when you left, that is if they hired someone." The detective followed Rand's gaze to the building. "Have you come up with any other possibilities?"

"No, I find it hard to believe it's anyone I know, even Reggie and Vanessa."

"The problem there is that the first attack was before they could have feasibly known about Kiley, unless of course that was just an accident." Gerome let it hang.

Rand rubbed his temple where a headache was beginning to form. "Let me know what you find."

"The moment we know something. You know, you should have let the EMT's look at your cheek. You could probably use a couple of stitches."

When they got back to Kiley, his mother was there too. She had an arm around Kiley with Mrs. Matthews still clucking over her. He was happy to see the acceptance between the two women most important in his life.

"Rand, your face," his mother exclaimed.

"It's nothing."

"Let's take a look at it over here." Dr. Matthews motioned to where his car had been parked. He led him away. "No reason to upset the ladies."

"Is Kiley all right?"

"Yes, just make sure she gets a good night's sleep." He opened the car and motioned for Rand to sit then removed his bag from the trunk. "It should have a stitch, but it's not worth going to the hospital, unless you'd rather have the plastic surgeon do it."

"If you can to it here, that'd be great."

"It won't take five minutes." Dr. Matthews proceeded to put two stitches in his face. "You can stop by my office or by your regular doctor's office in about six days and have them removed."

"Thanks, but Kiley is the one I'm worried about."

"Kiley is fine now that she knows you are. She was just as worried about you. I suggest a good night's sleep for both of you."

"That's what we were planning to do before this happened."

"Then do it, but take a couple of ibuprofen first. You'll be pretty sore."

"Like take two aspirin and call me in the morning."

"You can forget the call unless you start to feel sick. I will warn you, though. Tomorrow you will likely feel a lot worse."

Rand laughed dryly. "That's comforting. Right now I feel like I've been run over."

"Just a fair warning. Now, can we give you and that pretty wife of yours a ride home?"

Rand looked back at his car. "If you don't mind, I'd appreciate it. My mother will be tied up here awhile with the ball."

"Let's get the women then."

# Chapter Thirteen

Rand walked into the master bath, glancing at the mirror. "We're a pair. I just got stitches out of my arm, you get them in your forehead, you get them out this morning, and I get them tonight."

"I'd say it's a pattern we need to break." Kiley came up from behind him, sliding her arms around him and laying her cheek on his back. She was surprised at how natural the action seemed to be after such a short time.

"Agreed, I think what hurts more than the stitches and the car was I really liked this tux. It fit really well. Not like a straightjacket." He put his hands over hers holding her there.

"You looked great in it." She slid her hands up helping him remove the tattered garment. Kiley turned away only to turn back as he removed his shirt.

"Rand, your shoulder!"

Her fingers ran over the bruised flesh. When he flinched involuntarily, she jerked her hand back.

"It's all right," he turned to find tears trickling down her cheek. "Oh Kiley." He cradled her face in his hands, kissing away the tears.

"I just don't like to see you hurt."

"My little darling, how about you take me to bed and kiss it all better?" He led her from the room, turning off the lights so she couldn't see the bruises anymore.

CRSO

It was Rand's groan as he shifted in his sleep that woke Kiley late the next morning. Without thinking, she started to rise to get him something for the pain. She was halfway up when the nausea hit her. She fled to the bathroom.

When she came out, Rand was waiting with a wet washcloth. "I'm sorry, sweetheart." He kissed her forehead.

"For what?"

"For you being sick. It's entirely my fault."

Kiley's confusion softened to a smile. "I don't mind being sick. I mean, I don't like being sick. I'm not saying this right." She took a breath. "I like knowing your baby is growing in me. I want to have your baby," She kissed him to affirm her words. "Why don't you go soak you shoulder in the hot tub? I'll take a short swim then fix you something special for breakfast."

"Couldn't interest you in joining me in the hot tub?"

"Sorry, can't. The literature Dr. Matthews gave me cautioned about hot tubs. They're not good for the baby, it raises the body temperature and blood pressure and can stress the baby. I would say this little one has had enough stress as it is."

Rand stroked a finger down her cheek while looking deeply into her eyes. "You really don't mind this baby." He dropped his hand to run the same caress across her flat stomach.

"No, I love it."

"The morning sickness, tiredness, limits placed on you, not to mention what it will do to your body?"

"Well, since you mentioned it. How will you feel about me when I get so huge I waddle?"

He didn't try to fight back the grin. "I want to see you swelled with my baby. I want to know part of me is growing here." He patted her stomach. "I was wrong when I thought that I could produce the baby the way I planned. It was cold and calculated. I wouldn't have loved its mother, and I wouldn't have had these feelings. She would have been just another employee. I would have missed this love, the right and joy to be able to touch you. Kiley, sometimes I can't believe it happened but honestly, I love you," he declared. "The best thing that ever happened to me was that mistake in the doctor's office."

"I know, but I choose not to look at it as a mistake. I want to think it was destiny. That I was to be yours because, even after just a couple weeks, I can't imagine living without you." Tears welled up in her eyes, but Rand dried them with kisses and words of love.

∽∞

They were just finishing breakfast when Ryan Buchanan called asking Rand if he could come down to the District Attorney's office and see him. Rand had only been gone about twenty minutes when Ronnie called and asked if she could visit.

"Sure, I was just going out to the green house but that can wait until later."

"I could meet you there. I'd like to see what you're doing," Ronnie returned.

"Okay, I'll meet you there."

Kiley stopped to pulled her hair back into a ponytail and grab a handful of crackers before heading out the door. The short walk to the green house felt good. Kiley could hardly believe the progress that had been made on it. Even after seeing the blueprints it amazed her. Rand's little hot house was far more elaborate than she would have dreamed.

The concrete floor was in place, with the metal skeletal framing. Over half of the side panels had been installed with the hosing and tubes for water and air circulation. By next week, the tables would all be in place and ready for plants.

She shook her head. Rand didn't do things halfway. She stepped from the greenhouse to the smaller building being constructed next to it, which was to be her drying area and workshop.

It was mostly finished, even the tables and shelving were up. Windows circled around the structure letting in a lot of light from outside to work by. All the windows were screened so they could be opened.

Kiley remembered the night that she had told Rand she liked to work on her back porch because she liked the light and the fresh air. It was the second night Rand had been at her house. It seemed that Rand had never forgotten anything she had ever told him about her dreams, and he was doing his best to make them come true. She ran her finger over the table.

The sound of a car approaching drew her to the window. Ronnie's red Porsche pulled around to the other side of the green house.

"Ronnie, I'm in here," Kiley called making her way around the table toward the door, then froze. Instead of Ronnie, it was her sister who stepped into the doorway.

"Eloise. Sorry, I was expecting someone else."

"I know, Veronica, the little traitor, but she won't be here. The airhead is busy trying to find her keys."

"But you have them," Kiley said, feeling extremely uneasy.

"She will be so busy looking, she won't even notice her car gone. I'll be back and miraculously find her keys before she does. She can get here in time to find your body."

Kiley stepped back as Eloise brought her hand out from behind the doorframe. One of the shovels left there by the workmen was held in her gloved hand. Kiley felt sick at the realization Eloise meant to kill her with it.

"Why?" She couldn't help asking though she knew the answer – the will.

"Why? Because you have caused nothing but trouble. If you would have been scared off or taken the money

Reggie offered, none of this would've been necessary. But it's already too late, isn't it! You're already pregnant."

When Kiley tried to talk, Eloise cut her off. "Don't deny it. I saw you at the ball last night, watching the presentation. The way you touched your stomach, the way Rand followed the motion and looked. You know, I think Rand really does want it and you. But that's even better. After your death, he'll be in mourning and not even think to replace you. Time will pass and we can get rid of Roe Technology." Eloise walked slowly into the room.

"I don't understand, why are you doing this if you just want to sell it? You have plenty of money."

"You don't understand. My mother stayed married to that old man for almost five years. He wouldn't even give Reggie a decent position. If he had, Reggie wouldn't have gotten into money problems with gambling. He's meeting with the District Attorney now, but you know that since Rand is with them."

"Reggie is in on this?"

"Are you kidding? Reggie doesn't have the stomach. That's why he never stood up to the old man," the woman said bitterly.

"And Ronnie?" Kiley had to know.

"Ronnie is so excited to have a friend that she can't seem to realize you're just helping Rand."

"You're wrong, I am Ronnie's friend. She is nice and I like her." Kiley felt a need to defend her.

"You would. Well, you won't have to worry about her." Eloise raised the shovel.

"You can't just kill me."

"You might think that, but I know different." She swung the shovel, hitting the table not six inches from Kiley. "You should have left Rand when you could."

Kiley moved, but before she could make it around the table, Eloise swung again. Kiley barely dodged back away from the metal edge. She was forced behind the table. It was a standoff. Kiley couldn't get out, but Eloise couldn't get to her around the table without giving Kiley a chance to escape.

"You're just delaying the inevitable."

"If you think I'll go mildly, think again. I'm going to fight you."

The woman laughed, taking another swing. Kiley dodged back around. Eloise kept coming, taking grisly glee at forcing Kiley around the room.

A small sliver of hope rushed through Kiley when she noticed a section of two-by-four on the ground. She maneuvered her way toward it, but when she made the grab Eloise was there. Kiley snatched the board and dove out of the way. The hard metal missed her head but caught her thigh before she made it clear.

Kiley cried out in pain as she scrambled under the table. Half of her leg felt numb as she struggled to stand. Kiley was sure it wasn't broken, but it didn't want to hold her weight as she made her dash for the door.

Her escape was cut off about eight feet short as Eloise got there first. Eloise stared at her. A satisfied smile curved her lips. She swung the shovel at Kiley's head.

Kiley brought the board up, blocking the shovels descent. The jarring impact vibrated up her arm, almost making her lose hold of the board. Stumbling back, Kiley recovered in time to block the next strike.

Kiley almost went down. Eloise, too, stumbled back, giving Kiley enough room to make it around the table. They were back to where they started. A standoff on either side of the table, by this time they both gasped in air. Each waited for the other to make a move.

"Kiley!"

Kiley jerked as she heard Rand call her name just outside the door.

"Rand, look out!" Kiley yelled a warning, but it was too late.

He stepped through the door.

Her warning was enough though. Rand pulled back, alert enough to catch a glimpse of the shovel as it swung toward him. He ducked. It missed his head, but unfortunately hit the shoulder he'd landed on the night before.

A pained groan burst from his body. He dropped to his knees. His arm clutched to his body. He had no defenses as Eloise lifted the shovel over her head, the next blow intended for his head.

"No!" Kiley rushed forward, swinging the board like a baseball bat. She hit Eloise solidly in the stomach, knocking her back. The shovel hit the doorframe. Already loosened from the blow she received, the shovel fell harmlessly from Eloise's hands as the woman dropped to the floor.

Between sobs, Kiley made her way to Rand, who was trying to rise. Tears blurred her vision as he reached for her with one arm. The other stayed tight to his body. He pulled her to him, flinching when he shifted his shoulder, but didn't release her for a full minute as he kept an eye on Eloise who lay unmoving on the ground.

Knowing they had to call the police, he pulled back. "Shh." He raised a hand to brush back the tears from her cheek then tucked a lock of hair that had come free from her ponytail behind her ear. "It's over now."

He drew her out the door. They made their way together to Ronnie's Porsche to use the phone there. With the call complete, Rand wrapped his arm around her. They leaned back against the car together while waiting for the police.

"You found me," Kiley whispered against his neck.

"Ronnie called the house just as I got home. She was trying to tell you her keys and car were gone. She didn't want you waiting for her."

"Eloise stole them. She said Reggie was arrested or something."

"He's cutting a deal with the District Attorney's office. Ryan's trying to help him. Don't think about it now." He rested his head against hers.

Both startled and raised their heads as a horn blared from a black Mercedes tearing up the road, headed toward them. Rand shoved Kiley to the ground as he turned catching sight of Eloise as she once again came at them with the shovel.

Rand took Eloise down with a flying tackle before she could bring the shovel down. The two struggled on the ground. Even with Rand's injured shoulder, it was over quickly and he had Eloise pinned down.

Ronnie came running from the Mercedes to Kiley's side. "Are you all right?"

"Yes." She looked up to Rand then to the road as a police car pulled up.

As the police tried to handcuff Eloise, she went ballistic, yelling that Kiley couldn't have a baby. That the company was theirs. They put up with the old man. She screamed that Ronnie was a traitor, making her sister cry. Even after they read her her-rights and got her in the police car her tirade continued.

Rand drew Ronnie aside with Kiley and tried to shelter them.

Ronnie took a deep breath and wiped back her tears. "Mother is always complaining and saying that," she said dully, with sadness.

Kiley slid her arms around Ronnie.

Ronnie accepted the comforting gesture for a moment then straightened. "I better go tell Mother. She will want to get hold of an attorney right away. She's not going to accept this."

Kiley caught her hand. "Are you going to be all right?"

After a moment, Ronnie straightened and squeezed the hand back. "Yes, yes I will be," she said the words with new strength. "I'll come see you later."

Kiley nodded and watched her walk away.

Rand slid his arm back around Kiley from behind, pulling her back against him. "You know, I think she will be." He pressed a kiss against Kiley's neck. "Are you okay?"

She nodded.

"You're sure? I pushed you pretty hard."

"I'm all right. It's just hard to believe Eloise was trying to kill me. How could she even have found out about me before we got married?"

He shrugged. "She might have followed me. I'm just glad we have her, and you're safe now."

"I'll agree with that."

Two officers approached, and they were split up to go over what happened. They each signed the statements then assured they would come to the station later. They were told that Detective Gerome, for once, was off and that he would be contacting them later for the follow up, though it seemed pretty much open and shut especially with Eloise's ranting.

Kiley insisted on Rand having his shoulder checked. The X-rays showed no break, but with all the bruising, he was given a sling and instructed on taking care for the next couple days. They stopped at the police station to sign the forms and were just about to leave when Vanessa came in with her lawyer.

For a moment, Kiley thought the woman was going to make a scene. Rand must have thought the same thing, because he pulled her tight to him, but with a whispered word from her attorney, Vanessa glared, then turned away from them, with her nose high in the air.

# Chapter Fourteen

Two days later, Rand's secretary greeted Kiley warmly
the moment Kiley stepped in the office. Rand was in a
meeting, but his secretary opened his office so she could
wait inside. Kiley wandered around the room a few minutes
before sitting at his desk.

Peeking in his drawer, she removed a legal pad from it
and wrote 'I love you' on it and drew an elaborate border
around it with flowers and vines then placed it back in his
desk to find after she left. She'd just closed the drawer,
when the door opened.

"Hi." She smiled brightly.

"Hi." He shut the door coming forward. "I was kind of
hoping I'd find you on the couch when Beth said you were
in here."

"The door wasn't locked." Kiley heard the lock click
in answer to her comment and laughed. "Besides, I was
feeling the power of the chair." She swung side to side.

"Power, huh."

"Yeah."

"We'll have to see if we can give you the full effect
then." He came across the room and kissed her breathless.
Sometime during the kiss their places had shifted, and
when they finished Kiley sat in Rand's lap, held against
him while his hands stroked her back.

"I think I like the power of this chair." Kiley pressed a
kiss to his neck.

"What are you up to today?"

"Having lunch with you?" she said hopefully.

"That sounds good. I just have to reschedule my one o-clock with Floyd in marketing."

"I thought that was this morning."

"I had to reschedule."

"To help Ronnie. She called me and said she had come to see you. I can't believe Vanessa tried to disinherit and cut her off. Reggie and Eloise's problems aren't Ronnie's. Ronnie was the one that tried to do the right thing and save us."

"Vanessa is something. But we won't have to worry about her anymore. She can't keep Ronnie from her inheritance. Grandpa set up individual trusts so Vanessa has no say, never has for that matter, though Ronnie never knew that. Vanessa's been holding out on her. With the criminal charges against Eloise, her portion of the inheritance may be nullified. Vanessa has decided to move to Europe. She's not even going to wait for the trial. She's out to marry another rich husband."

"Is she going to sell the house?"

"She can't. It's not hers. All of the Monroe estate has been mine for a long time. She had the use of the house as long as she lived there but that's ending. I told Ronnie she could stay there as long as she wants."

"You're wonderful." Kiley kissed him.

"I've been taking lessons from my wife." He kissed her back soundly before they went to lunch.

"What are you doing for the rest of the day?" Rand asked as they left the table in the cafeteria.

"Well, I delivered my arrangements already this morning, but I still feel like being out, so I thought I'd go shopping. Look at furniture. Maybe something for the baby's room. I know it's early." She shrugged her shoulders and smiled.

"I think it's fine," he assured her.

"I'll show you if I find anything I like."

"Sounds good, I'll walk you to the car."

"You don't have to, I'm right out front and —" She reached up and straightened his tie. "— you're already late." Before he could object further, she stretched up and kissed him good-bye before escaping out of his arms.

"Do you have your phone?" he called after her.

Turning back, she slipped her hand in her jacket pocket and lifted it out for him to see. "Bye." She grinned, walking out the large glass doors. Kiley heard him laughing as the doors closed behind her.

The sun felt wonderful. She felt wonderful. Kiley glanced around at the shrubs in front of the building and wondered if Rand would let her plant some flowers around them. She especially wanted to plant some flowers around back where there was an outside eating area. It was nice but could use a little brightening up.

Kiley reached the rental car she was driving, unlocked it and slid in. Closing the door, she put the key in the ignition. At that moment, she realized two things were wrong. The window on the back passenger side was broken out and there was the strong smell of expensive men's cologne filling the car that was not there earlier.

Kiley fumbled for the unfamiliar door handle when a single word made her freeze.

"Don't!" The cold metal of a gun barrel rested against the back of her head. It wasn't until she looked in the mirror that she connected the voice and the smell of cologne with the man she could hardly believe was in the seat behind her. Dr. Harvey leaned forward with the gun pressed to her head.

"Very carefully, start the car and put it in gear. I want you to drive out of the parking lot. You will do nothing to draw attention to yourself. If you do, you will die and so will whoever is around. To reinforce his words, he jabbed the gun against her skull.

Doing as she was told, she headed for the gate. When Harvey slid down so not to be seen, Kiley hesitated a moment.

"Don't even think about it. The gun is pointed right at your stomach. That cursed seed will be the first to go."

Terror shot through Kiley.

Pasting a smile on her face, she tried to remain calm as she waved and drove past the guard booth. She knew once away from people she was likely as good as dead, but she couldn't let anyone else get hurt. Besides, she had to stall for time until she could think of a way to get help or away.

Pulling to a stop at a red light she felt Harvey breathing down her neck. Her eyes were searching for help when she noticed the ad on the bus stop bench for phone calls. With a mental thank you, she slid her hand in her pocket. Moving her fingers by feel, she prayed she pressed the right place to recall the last number dialed, which she knew was Rand.

&#x03B;&#x3D0;

The first thing Rand saw when the elevator door opened to the executive level was Detective Gerome and another officer.

"Gerome, this is an unexpected surprise." Rand stuck out his hand to shake the detective's. "The officer did say you'd be in touch to do a follow up."

"May I speak with you a moment?"

The serious tone in the detective's voice made Rand uneasy. "I have an appointment, but I can put it off awhile. Beth, will you call Floyd and have him hold on until I call?" Rand motioned the men to his office.

They were hardly inside when Gerome started to speak. "Do you know where your wife is?"

"Kiley was just here. We had lunch together." Rand felt the tentacles of alarm tighten around him. "What's wrong?" He glanced at the other officer then back to Gerome. "What is it?"

"We got the information on the car abandoned in the hit and run. It was sold two weeks ago. The name given was faked. The person was in the hospital at the time. It was paid for in cash. The salesman noticed some things about the man, like hat, aviator glasses and the fact that he wore expensive shoes and a leather jacket that was worth about half of what the car was.

"The car was extremely clean, but we did find a print, a partial thumb. We checked it against Reggie's, no match. So we ran it in hopes it was enough and got lucky. It came back with a match, an old malpractice suit in Oregon. The man was arrested, but charges were dropped. There was a big scandal about six years back. It seems that through negligence of a doctor, the sperm specimen was destroyed. Then, to hide the fact, he used his own sperm to impregnate the woman."

"Norman Harvey," Rand said feeling sick.

"Correct."

"How could charges be dropped? How could he …"
Rand couldn't get more out.

"It's interesting. The husband had died and had left semen. The wife decided she still wanted to have his baby. Anyway, after the suit was filed, she was killed in an accident and the suit fell through. The thing is —" he paused. "The accident —she slipped and fell in front of a car."

"Kiley."

Gerome nodded. "Harvey also has a red Porsche registered to him."

Rand reached for the phone and punched Kiley's number, but it was busy. "Why?" He wasn't really asking the question, but Gerome answered. "I'd say it was simple. Man with an enormous ego has a large problem. He impregnated the wrong woman. The suit could be horrendous, especially with a high profile name like yours attached. It would destroy him."

ALYSIA S. KNIGHT

"But I didn't want the publicity. In fact, I was so busy trying to win Kiley and then so happy to have her, I hadn't given him any thought. I don't think Kiley ever thought of pressing charges either. It isn't in her nature to sue."

"A guy like Harvey wouldn't have considered that. All he would have thought was how much he had to lose.

Rand nodded and pushed the dial again. "Still busy."

"Mr. Monroe," his secretary opened the door. "I'm sorry to disturb you, but there's a strange call on your private line. I was going to disconnect it, but I think that it's your wife. I sent it over."

Rand pushed the speaker. There was silence on the line then Kiley's voice. "Where shall I go?" There was no missing the tremor in her voice.

"Turn right at the light." They could hardly make out the male voice.

"At the pancake house?"

"Yes."

"We're getting on the freeway?"

"Yes."

"North or south?"

"North," the man snapped.

There was a few seconds of silence then Kiley's apology. "Sorry, I'm still unfamiliar with the rental car Rand got me until we decide on a new one."

"You said that earlier."

"Yes, sorry, I'm frightened."

"Well, be quiet." The man's voice was full of aggravation. The phone fell silent.

Gerome motioned to Rand to move away from the desk and phone. They joined the secretary by the door. "Is there any way you can transfer that call to another phone?" he asked in a whisper.

Beth nodded. "I can conference call it to Mr. Monroe's cell phone."

"Great. What about possibilities of recording the conversation."

"My micro recorder I use for notes," Rand suggested. Gerome nodded.

Rand went back to his desk carefully removing the recorder from the drawer. He activated it and placed it by the phone when Kiley spoke again.

"How far are we going?"

"A ways, don't worry. I'll let you know."

Rand heard Kiley whimper and clenched his fist. It was all he could do to move away from the phone, but he didn't dare be too close when his phone rang.

The moment the call was connected to his cell phone, Rand pushed mute and headed for the door. "Beth stay with the recorder and other phone. Make sure you shut that door so no sounds get in."

"Stay with the secretary." Gerome told the other officer before hurrying after Rand. "Where are you going?"

"With you, after my wife."

"You should stay here. Let the police handle it."

"Would you?" When Gerome didn't answer, he continued. "Did you really expect me to?"

"No," Gerome conceded as the elevator door opened.

"Then come on."

Rand jogged through the lobby with Gerome beside him.

Gerome's car was an unmarked police car, but he had a flasher on the dash. He turned it on but left the siren off as they headed for the northbound freeway.

൭൸

Traffic began to slow around them. Kiley glanced down at the phone she concealed between her and the door. The light showed there was still a connection. She felt a little hope.

"The traffic is slowing. There must be an accident on the northbound road," she added a little stress to northbound. "Do you want me to get off?"

The man behind her fidgeted, craning his neck from side to side to see what was happening. Kiley tried to relax, bringing her hand from the steering wheel to shield the phone.

"Stay on," he ordered. "It's clear up ahead." Then he grabbed the back of her hair, yanking her head back.

Kiley let out a little cry and jerked the wheel. Luckily they had slowed to only seventeen miles an hour.

"Both hands on the wheel," he snapped. When she gripped the wheel with the other hand, he gave another yank. "Don't try that again. Remember where this gun is pointed. Even if you didn't die, the baby surely would."

"Why are you doing this?" Kiley couldn't help crying.

"Why do you think? I'm not going to risk everything – my degree, my reputation – all because of a stupid blackout? It wasn't my fault. The lights were out. You were in the wrong place. I couldn't risk Monroe's sperm. I was efficient. I was doing the right thing. It was you that messed up," he ranted. "Got pregnant, a virgin. I can just hear what people would say. No matter what good you try to do. They wouldn't see it that way. They'd turn on me. Why couldn't you die like the last time?"

Kiley felt a chill run through her.

"I didn't have to do anything. It was a simple push and she was gone. But you didn't die."

Kiley swallowed her throat going dry. The man behind her with a gun had gone completely insane.

"I ... I wouldn't have caused problems. I want this baby. I married Rand Monroe. I love him." Her words grew stronger with more conviction. "This is the best thing that ever happened to me."

"Shut up! I don't trust you."

Ahead, the road cleared as they passed the cars off the side of the road. The speed increased.

"We're passed the accident. It doesn't look too bad, thankfully." Kiley made the comment, which he ignored.

Fifteen minutes later, Harvey ordered her to get off the freeway. Kiley repeated the exit number aloud as she turned off, heading up in the hills. After they passed a couple of small towns, there was no more traffic.

She started to worry about losing the connection, but the light on the phone beside her indicated it was still good. Kiley tried to imagine Rand on the other end, racing toward her. He would come after her. It was just if he got there in time. She wanted to grab up the phone and hear his voice.

"Turn here." The doctor's voice startled her.

"Where? There's no road." Kiley actually caught a glimpse of it as they passed but pretended otherwise.

"You missed it. Back up."

Kiley stopped, shifted in reverse and backed up slowly. "Oh, I missed it because of those two pine trees and that yellow bush."

"I was thinking of building a cabin up here, but you seemed to like the outdoors so much I decided you'd like to be buried here instead."

"Dr. Harvey, you don't have to do this." Kiley tried pleading, knowing her time was up and no one was there to help. "I won't say anything. Rand won't either. You're sworn to help people."

"Pull over," he directed.

Fear speared through Kiley. Instead of complying, she slammed her foot on the gas. The car shot forward. She thought of ramming a tree, but thinking of the baby, she rejected it as not worth the risk, so she braced herself and slammed on the brakes and pulled the car hard to the right.

The car spun then jerked to a stop. Kiley, who was prepared and wearing her seatbelt, remained upright. Harvey, who hadn't done up his seatbelt and was sitting forward on the edge of his seat, was thrown across the car into the door and onto the floor.

Kiley didn't waste any time to check on him. She pushed open the door. Her legs were shaky but held as she ran for the trees. Dropping down behind some bushes, she scrambled out of sight. Being as still as possible, she waited almost a minute before she heard Harvey emerge from the car.

He swore. "Come out. You can't hide." His voice sounded pitiful. He swore again. Kiley heard a twig snap and some bushes rustling a ways away. He was coming her way. She pressed flat into the rich, moist soil, willing herself to remain absolutely silent. Her heart pounded so loud she feared he'd hear it.

He paused within ten feet of her then turned back toward the car. In the distance, she heard the roar of a car engine and debated making a run for the road, but she knew she would never make it before Harvey saw her. She didn't know what kind of a shot he was, but she wasn't going to risk it. She'd stay hidden until he gave up and left, then, when it was safe, she'd walk to help. It might take time, but she would be safe, and Rand would be looking for her.

The roar of the engine drew closer, then came the sound of tires skidding to a stop.

"Freeze Harvey. Drop the gun and put your hands up."

A shot rang out followed immediately by two more. There was a moment of total silence in the woods.

"Kiley!"

She jumped at the sound of Rand's voice. Believing she was hearing things, she didn't answer until Rand's voice came again, yelling her name over and over.

"Rand." It came out as a whisper. A branch pulled at her hair as she worked her way free from under the bushes. "Rand," she called, this time louder. She could hear someone running toward her.

"Kiley." Rand reached her in time to haul her to her feet. Even before she was steady, she launched herself into his arms. He was ready to catch her, pulling her tight. "I was afraid we were too late."

Fevered hands ran over her body. A hard kiss devoured her lips. She didn't complain, clinging to every bit of life he made her feel, sweeping away her fears.

"Monroe, is she all right?"

"She's wonderful." He kissed her. "Incredible." He kissed her again. "Brilliant."

The sound of more cars approaching drew them apart and toward the cars. Rand kept her snug to his side. "Come on."

People swarmed the clearing when Rand and Kiley made it through the trees.

"Don't look." Rand turned her away from where Harvey lay on the ground, two medics worked on him.

"Is he alive?" Her voice trembled as she pressed into Rand.

"Yes." It was Gerome who answered, coming up to them. "It's hard to say if he'll make it to the hospital, though. We'll need another statement, but it will just be a formality. We recorded the conversation. I already spoke to the officer with your secretary." He looked at Rand. "She got it all and it came out clear." He turned his attention back to Kiley. "I have to congratulate you. That was smart thinking. You did good."

"I wanted Rand." Tears welled up in her eyes. "Dr. Harvey broke out the back window. I didn't notice until it was too late." She started to cry.

Rand pulled her against his chest. "Shh, sweetheart, this time it is really all over." He looked up at Gerome. "Can you get us out of here?"

"Yeah, I'm under suspension while they investigate the shooting."

Kiley lifted her head, staying in Rand's arms. "But you saved me."

"It's just procedure, nothing to worry about. He shot first, but it has to be cleared. Shall we take you home now?"

"Yes, please." She looked back to Dr. Norman Harvey. "It's sad. It really was all for nothing. All I want is Rand and this baby." Tears slipped from her eyes as Rand pressed his lips to her temple. Kiley looked to her husband.

"I love you." His voice was thick with feeling.

"I love you." She turned into him.

"Forever." He tightened his hold. She could only nod, the feeling too thick in her heart.

# About the Author

I grew up in a small town in Wyoming loving the outdoors, sports, art, and reading Hardy Boys books. After reading them all at least a half dozen times, I started writing my own stories.

For thirty-three years I was married a wonderful, honorable man. I'm mother of five children and grandmother of nine, eight boys and one girl. I love traveling. Through my husband's work and vacations, I have visited much of the United States, all over Europe, Canada, Mexico, China, Thailand, Cambodia and Australia, giving me many intriguing locations and experiences for my stories.

I am a storyteller. I write the classic hero story because I think there's a need for more heroes, love, and adventure in our lives. I'm not out to change the world with my writing; I'm just hoping to make your day a little better.

Hope you enjoy.
Alysia S. Knight

Please feel free to visit me through my website:

www.alysiasknight.com